TO HAVE AND TO HOLD

Jeremiah 29:11 KJV

[11] For I know the thoughts that I think toward you, saith the LORD, thoughts of peace, and not of evil, to give you an expected end.

Taiwo Iredele Odubiyi

PRAISES FOR THE BOOKS OF TAIWO IREDELE ODUBIYI

Pastor Taiwo Iredele Odubiyi is a prolific writer with an uncommon grace. When I first picked up her book *This Time Around* several years ago, I knew she was an author whose work I would follow for a very long time. I have followed her work closely for over eighteen years now, and I can truly say that she's God's gift to this generation. Her stories are real page-turners that are not only relatable but life transforming. An encounter with any of her books would not only educate and enlighten you but would also reveal the mind of God to you on issues relating to marriage and relationships, both with men and especially with God. I pray that the Lord continues to strengthen Pastor Taiwo, and may He multiply His grace and wisdom upon her life in Jesus' name, Amen! … thank you for blessing us with *One Day in December* too. I was thoroughly blessed by it.
- Tumise Falana, USA

I remembered reading "Love Fever" during CRK class then in secondary school. Mama (the teacher) *carry my matter go staff room to escalate o* 😄. I can never forget. I thank God for our teacher that intervened that I was reading a Christian novel. They passed it from one teacher to another before I could get back the novel.
- Adesinuola Ayomiposi Muritala, Nigeria

To think that I have been searching for this woman's page for a long time now! Thanks for blessing us with your books.
- Akinlawon Theresa, Nigeria

I have always loved *Mama* Taiwo Iredele's novels way back in secondary school. I remember how my friends and I used to compete in reading her novels... 😊 The way Mama combines Christianity and romance in stories is not from this planet! The likes of 'Love on the pulpit', and so on... More grace!
- Alabi Vivian

Alabi Vivian is very correct. I read all of Pastor Taiwo Iredele Odubiyi's novels until I stopped receiving notifications about the newest edition. I even sold some then. She is an amazing storyteller.
- Bukola Shope, Nigeria

Wow! I have been your follower for more than 10 years now. *Love on the Pulpit* was one of my favorites of your books. GOD BLESS your brain more, *l'oruko JESU KRISTI, ÀMÍN.* 🙏🙏🙏 *- Yemmy Oceon, Nigeria*

Wow! My best author back then in secondary school. I still have: *Love fever, shadows from the past, in love for us, this time around, oh baby, you found me, and too much of a good*

thing. How can I restock my library with more of your books?
- *Jumoke Adetayo Olanrewaju, Nigeria*

Ohhh Jesus!!! These books that I used to read back then! How can I get all your books please? It's been a while, Christ!
- *Atobatele Titilayomi Ike Poju, Nigeria*

I just finished reading *Too much of a good thing* this morning. Wow! I really love how you put the story into play wish every Bible story would be written in such manner. I got understanding of some things that I didn't know before, even though I had read the story many times in the Bible. Now I'm rushing to go and read *What changed you?* 😊 Kudos to you ma. More grace in Jesus' name. I just needed to comment on this book because as I was reading it, it was *sweeting* me 🤩
- *Adegoke Blessing Jesutomi, Offa, Kwara State, Nigeria*

Oh baby! was the first novel I read. I never knew Christian novels can be so interesting, educational and spiritual till I read Pastor Taiwo Odubiyi's books
- *Funmilola Omolola*

That was where I first saw your book (*Love Fever*). The Spirit of the LORD in me convicted me of so many things and I stopped reading Harlequin and secular romance novels.

I have read:
Too much of a good thing (I have a copy),
In love for us (Gave someone and it hasn't been returned),
Tears on my pillow (I have a copy, and I have read it up
to 8 times),
My desire (I have it),
Love fever (I have it),
Rescued by Victor (I purchased one for my cousin),
With this ring (a friend gifted me!),
Love on the pulpit (I have one),
Shadows from the past (I have a copy),
My first love (I have one),
No one is a nobody (I purchased it for my cousin),
This time around (I have it),
The forever kind of love (I bought it on Okadabooks App),
Oh baby! (Presently rereading it!),
Billy the bully (I purchased it for my loved ones),
If you could see me now (I have it),
Marriage on fire (I have it),
Sea of regrets (have it),
God's words to singles (I have it),
When a man loves a woman (I have it),
To love again (My cousin bought it from me),
You found me (I think I have it!)
- Aramide Oluwa, Nigeria

Your books are spirit-lifting. After reading one, I always
anticipate reading another. Your style of scripting words

together is so exceptional. Always love reading your books.
More grace.
- James Olaoluwa Asu, Ikorodu, Lagos, Nigeria

I enjoyed reading your books in my secondary school days.
They were quite enlightening, inspiring and easy to read and
comprehend.
- Christiana Ogundare, Nigeria

ACKNOWLEDGMENTS

I thank You, Lord God, the I AM, my Rescuer and Lord, For:

Yet another book. *Thank You for the great privilege and grace that You have given me to speak and write for You, and about You: about Your will, Your ways, Your word, and Your wondrous love. Thank You for the mercy You have shown me to know You,*

All the wonderful family members You have blessed me with – *for all that they do, and for always being there for me,*

This book's editor, Babatope Olabode. *I appreciate your meticulous attention to detail, patience, and valuable suggestions. I'd also like to say a big 'God bless you' to you for believing in this ministry and your unwavering support. When I contacted you some time ago to know if you'd have time to edit my latest work, you told me "You're always preapproved." That means a lot to me,*

Families, friends, fans, and my avid readers - those who have been with me since the beginning of this great journey, and those who joined along the way, reading my books, supporting, praying, and encouraging me,

Lord, let those who read this book experience Your touch, transformation, and blessings, that they may know You are the real Author and that Your love and mercy truly endure forever!

It's All About You!　　　**Taiwo Iredele Odubiyi**

EXCERPTS

… They continued talking and then he asked, "So, is there a man who wouldn't be pleased that I'm talking to you?"

Adesua's voice came through with a laugh. "Just ask if I'm in a relationship."

They both laughed.

"So?" He pressed, smiling. …

… "I met a man at a time, whom I thought might be the right one for me, but shortly after we met, he began to complain that I worked with men and was too busy for his liking. He said he wasn't sure I wouldn't cheat on him, which I found very ridiculous. Some women may cheat on their spouses, but that's one thing I'll never do."

Tade smiled, his eyes never leaving hers. "Why have you brought this up?" …

… He also told her, "I know you're used to taking control because of the nature of your job. It's a trait I appreciate. But in our relationship, I want you to tone it down and trust me to handle things. If I'm not there, feel free to do whatever you need to do, but with me, I'd want you to enjoy being my wife."

She smiled, happy. "Okay, thank you." …

DEDICATION

To God

&

The TV personalities who have bravely retraced their steps to align their lives with the will of God, thereby inspiring others to do the same.

CHAPTER 1

ADESUA ARRIVED AT her parents' house where she lived, and honked the horn. Within seconds, the gateman threw the house's black gate wide open, and as she drove her car inside the compound, she greeted the thirty-something-year-old man.

The day was Monday, the last day of October, and the dashboard in her car showed that the time now was 8.40pm. She had just returned from JKITV studio and would be praying with two of her friends over the phone soon, at 9pm.

Quickly parking her silver-sky metallic Toyota RAV4 car beside her mother's black Nissan Altima, she grabbed her handbag and bunch of keys which included the car remote. Exiting the car, she closed the door, and when she pressed the remote, the car beeped as it locked.

While she walked up the slate walkway to the front door of the four-bedroom bungalow, she selected a key from the bunch in her hand. At the door, she inserted the key to unlock it, and stepped inside the cool interior of the house. Her parents and her immediate younger sister, Efua, were in the large, air-conditioned living room, relaxing. The TV was on.

As she walked in, she greeted them with a warm smile and announced that she had to pray with her friends now.

As Adesua went in the direction of her bedroom, she took her phone and called the two friends, Nancy and Moyo, to let them know she was now at home and ready to pray.

In her room, she turned on the overhead light and air conditioner, put the phone on speaker, and set it down on her well laid queen-size bed. After taking off her shoes and changing from her yellow skirt suit into a more comfortable home dress, she climbed into bed and lay on her back.

With her head resting on one pillow and the phone on another, the prayer session began with a worship song led by Moyo.

Moyo, Nancy and Adesua were members of *God's Word Assembly,* the church where they met and formed a close friendship.

Moyo, a lawyer, worked in a prestigious law firm where she was doing well. Her father was late, but before he died six years ago, Moyo was aware that her parents did not have a good marriage. Her father had once held a stable job and life seemed fine until he began gambling and frequently came home drunk. He eventually lost the job.

About six months later, he got a new job with a significantly lower salary. This did not matter much to the family though, as he hadn't been contributing financially at home since he began drinking and gambling and had left the running of the house to his wife. Moyo's mother, who worked full-time and had started a business, took on the responsibility of managing the household, paying bills, and providing for the family. The woman wasn't a Christian at the time; but she did these things in a bid to keep her family together.

He frequently borrowed money from his wife, and even though he never paid back, she continued to give him money, with the hope that he would come to his senses on time and become the man she once loved and married. Things did not improve however, and the financial burden became heavier on her. She began to borrow money from friends and family to pay her children's school fees, with a promise to pay back at the end of the month when she got her salary. There were times when she took out one loan to repay another, just to avoid embarrassment.

For a long time, she hid the challenges in her marriage from the children, wanting to shield them from sadness and resentment toward their father. Though she was deeply unhappy, she put on a brave face, determined to protect them.

Over the years, she told the children that their father was the one paying their school fees and providing for them. Now that she was a Christian, she realized that was a lie. While her intention was good, her method was wrong. She shouldn't have deceived her children, as it could lead to them doubting her in the future.

Her children later on discovered that what she told them was not true. As they grew older, they started to notice discrepancies and began asking her direct questions.

One day, as they were gathered in the living room, Moyo looked at her with a serious expression. "Mom, we've seen some things that don't add up. Was Dad really the one supporting us?"

She took a deep breath, knowing it was time to be honest. "I've been trying to protect you from the challenges in our lives," she said quietly. "But now that you're older, it's important for you to know the truth."

Moyo's eyes were filled with concern. "Does he have another family outside?"

She shook her head slowly. "No, I don't think so. As far as I know, he hasn't added adultery to his many problems."

In University, Moyo faced significant challenges. Each semester, paying her tuition was a struggle, and there were moments when she nearly had to drop out. To make ends meet, she started working on the side to cover her expenses.

She was in her final year when her father passed away, and as the family made preparations for his burial, she promised herself that she would not let any man cause her the same troubles her father had caused her mother. She vowed to work hard, earn her own money, and ensure that her finances remained under her control. Her money would be her money.

It was shortly after her father's burial that Moyo became a Christian and joined a campus fellowship. Few months after, she graduated from university, passed her bar exam, and was fortunate to secure a position at a law firm almost immediately. She still worked in the law firm, building a career.

Moyo now attended *God's Word Assembly* and belonged to the Greeters Department, but, she still struggled with the lingering pain from her past. Memories of financial struggles and the difficulties her father caused the family often resurfaced, leaving her upset. The promise she made to herself—to never let a man bring her the same troubles—still remained firmly in her mind.

When she began working at the law firm, Moyo made another significant promise to herself: to take care of her mother. This new commitment was a way for Moyo to reward her mother for all that she had endured. Her mother became a Christian two years ago.

Nancy worked for an international company. She secured the job a few months earlier and earned a good salary. Her parents both had good jobs which provided the family with a relatively comfortable lifestyle. Her parents who attended an orthodox church were not born again. Before Nancy became a Christian, she and her siblings went with their parents to the church.

Though Nancy's parents were still together, they lived more like co-tenants. They got married because her mother became pregnant with her. Growing up, Nancy noticed that her mother was sometimes very disrespectful to her father, calling him names. Nancy was young, but she knew the behavior was wrong. It also seemed that the woman cared more for her children than her husband.

Nancy was about eighteen years old when she realized she rarely saw her father, but she and her siblings assumed his absence was due to work, as their mother had explained. Some months later, however, they discovered he was having an affair with a woman who worked at a restaurant he frequented.

Outraged, Nancy's mother wanted to leave with her children, but their father pleaded for reconciliation. He told his wife he wanted to keep his marriage and children. Reluctantly, Nancy's mother stayed, but things had not been the same since. She claimed to have forgiven him, but her actions told a different story. She also said she believed her husband was still cheating on her, but she had chosen to ignore it. He could do whatever he liked as far as she was concerned. Now, as she told her family and friends, she was in the marriage for the sake of her children and comfort. Nancy and her siblings prayed and hoped they would have a better marriage than that.

Adesua had heard from Moyo and Nancy these details about their parents' marriages many times. Recognizing the significant impact that parents' marriage can have on children, she was grateful to God that her own parents who were Christians, were doing well. They had built a good life together and had been good parents to her and her sisters.

Adesua's parents were financially comfortable, and she appreciated them for the comfort and stability they provided for her and her sisters. She was well aware that she and her sisters had enjoyed certain benefits all their lives which many of their cousins and friends had not.

Her parents' marriage was also stable. Whenever she reflected on this, she admired her father for his wise choices, patience, and unwavering commitment to his wife and children. Even before he became a Christian, he had never been unfaithful or abusive to his wife, and after his conversion, he embraced and upheld a life of godliness. It wasn't as if he and his wife didn't have misunderstandings, but he chose to be patient, show love, and maintain peace. He had seen how some men destroyed their families by making wrong decisions and being harsh with their wives. He didn't want that. His wife was not perfect, but he had come to realize that she was better than many women, as he often remarked.

Adesua also appreciated her mother for her steadfast support for her father and for demonstrating to her what it meant to be a godly wife. The woman respected her husband, cooperated with him, allowed him to be the head of the home, and forgave him whenever he offended her.

Adesua's parents met in the US. Her father, Oze, was a law student at the time. Oze was an only child, and his rich parents wanted him to study abroad. He had a student visa and even though his parents sent money to him, he worked a few hours on campus so he could earn some money and be more comfortable.

He met his wife, Ese, a nurse, at a hospital during a routine medical checkup. The biracial lady was the nurse assigned to him, and their conversation sparked when he discovered she was half Nigerian. They connected over their shared background and exchanged phone numbers before he was discharged. Even though he was quiet and reserved, he had no problem talking to her that day.

They quickly became friends, and he discovered that he was a year older than her, she was a US citizen, and her mother who was from Edo State in Nigeria, lived in the US.

Oze was also from Edo State in Nigeria. He was tall, big, and dark in complexion while Ese was of average height and light brown in complexion. Ese's mother had had an affair with an American man she worked with in Nigeria, became pregnant, and gave birth to Ese. The white man did not marry her, but it was through his influence that the woman and her daughter, Ese, relocated to the US. Ese was two years old at the time of the relocation, and she and her mother soon became US citizens. Ese's mother later met a man in the US whom she married, and they had a son together.

As their friendship deepened, Ese discovered that even though Oze was big, strong, and hardworking, he was also incredibly generous, kindhearted, and easygoing—the qualities she had always sought in a man she would like to marry.

Oze and Ese fell deeply in love and soon became inseparable. As their relationship blossomed, they both knew they wanted to spend the rest of their lives together. Though they wished to marry, they decided to wait until Oze graduated a year later.

Oze made it clear to Ese that he would remain in the US for a while but would eventually return to Nigeria. They discussed it at length and Ese expressed her willingness to relocate with him. She trusted him and believed she would be alright with him in Nigeria. He would protect her.

Oze graduated from law school with flying colors, and once he passed his bar exams, he and Ese quickly set a wedding date. They began to make preparations, and Oze's parents traveled from Nigeria to celebrate this significant milestone.

Ese got pregnant with Adesua quickly. She also filed for her husband and Oze became a US citizen. She continued her job as a nurse but resigned when she became pregnant with their second daughter, Efua.

Oze joined an already established law firm, to gain experience and understand the legal landscape before launching out to start his own law practice which was his dream. He was there for about three years, and then, he took the leap. He rented a small office and established his own law firm, specializing in Commercial Law.

While he dedicated himself to growing the business, Ese stayed at home. She managed the home front, taking care of their children. She also encouraged and supported Oze, which meant a lot to him.

Before long, they purchased a house which was not far from her mother's house so they could easily drop off their children whenever it was necessary. This arrangement strengthened their family ties and allowed them to balance work and home life effectively.

Before long, they welcomed their third daughter, Enoredia, affectionately shortened to Noredia.

As Oze's law firm picked up, he started sending money to his parents in Nigeria. He wanted them to help him build two houses: one bungalow in a safe and nice residential neighborhood where he and his family would live when they finally relocated. The second structure would have two floors, with plans to use one for his law firm and rent out the other. Oze envisioned this as a way to establish his roots in Nigeria while ensuring a stable future for his family.

While the two houses were being constructed in Nigeria, Oze and his family continued with their lives in the US.

He hired two lawyers to join his firm and began training them to ensure they could effectively manage the office in his absence. He focused on instilling his vision and values in them, preparing the team for a smooth transition and continued success. He intended to stay connected with the office by phone and visit as needed.

Eventually, the moment came, and he packed up his family for the move back to Nigeria, excited to start this new chapter in their lives.

Adesua was sixteen at the time.

The family quickly settled down in Nigeria. Oze established his law firm which was now one of the prestigious law firms around. Oze and Ese's cars, and the two houses they owned, were a testimony of his success. The family didn't live extravagantly but lived nicely, as Oze didn't believe in wasting money.

The house they lived in, which was in a quiet neighborhood, was not luxurious, but it was tastefully furnished in a way that showed sophistication. The bungalow had a black roof, and the exterior was painted custard yellow while the windowsills and some parts of it were painted white. Its large living room was painted white and had a high ceiling. The furniture included elegant chandeliers, some décor pieces of high quality, elegant window curtains, beautiful artworks, and family portraits which adorned a side of the walls.

Ese would have loved to showcase their wealth, but she chose to abide by her husband's idea of living a simple life.

Oze and Ese got married about twenty nine years ago when he was twenty seven and she was twenty six. Now fifty six and fifty five respectively, they were still in love, respected each other, and spent time together.

Their three daughters were University graduates and doing well. Oze was perfectly content without a son. He loved his daughters and did not consider seeking a son with another woman. He could have done so, and he had opportunities to do so, but he chose not to. He knew the trouble that taking such a wrong step could bring into his life and home, and because he gave his family peace, he had peace as well. There was no time he reflected on this that he did not remember Ephesians 5:28 that states *he who loves his wife loves himself*.

❤ CHAPTER 2

ADESUA, SLIM, LIGHT SKINNED, and tall, looked like a model. She had inherited her father's height, but her rich, smooth, and fair complexion clearly came from her mother.

She would be twenty eight on November 12. Having been born in the United States of America and having spent the first sixteen years of her life there before coming to Nigeria with her family, she had American accent.

After graduating from the university with a degree in journalism, she worked for about three months before returning to pursue her MBA.

Adesua's life was very different from her sisters who were both medical doctors. She was a TV presenter.

Her work as a TV presenter was a dream come true for her. As a young girl, she loved watching talk shows and loved some of the hosts. As she watched them, she dreamed of having her own show when she grew up.

Before long, she began practicing by playing make-believe in her bedroom or the living room, entertaining her family who laughed and sometimes responded to whatever she was talking about. This built up her confidence. With time, her family began to encourage her and she put herself out more. In High School, she participated in school debates which helped her gain a lot of experience and more determination to pursue her dreams.

As a presenter with her own show at JKITV, her work included reporting on events, presenting information, and interviewing guests on topics such as spirituality and social issues.

Another thing she loved to do was act. She practiced acting roles at home when she was young and acted in some plays when she was in university. She planned to land an acting role in a movie before long, as several producers had already been reaching out to her.

She was happy that her parents supported her career choice and gave her financial support. When she just started her own show, she wasn't making much money, but she stayed and continued, without having to worry about how long she would be able to survive, or how her needs would be met. Her parents were there for her.

She loved her career and felt very fortunate that it had taken off, providing her with a good income. It also gave her the chance to meet influential people and attend exciting events which she liked.

She and her younger sisters were not yet married and still lived with their parents. Now, Adesua could afford to rent her own place and had considered it at a time but decided against it as she was comfortable in her parents' house. She had a room to herself, and the room which was fairly large, had its own bathroom and toilet. She had it decorated to her own taste, and the light pink colored room exuded elegance.

Aside from being comfortable in the house, living with her parents allowed her to save on rent and afford vacations abroad more easily. Although her parents didn't ask her for money, she chose to contribute monthly for groceries.

The parents were the first to become Christians in the family, which happened few months after they returned to Nigeria. Next to become Christians were Noredia, Efua, and finally Adesua, at the age of eighteen.

Oze and Ese were happy that their children were also Christians and did not mess around. The family members worshipped in the same church—Solid Rock Bible Church—until about three years ago when Adesua pulled out to join *God's Word Assembly*. She did so because she liked the church's location, and liked the fact that the church was air-conditioned, and filled with young professionals.

Oze and Ese didn't mind Adesua's decision as they believed that the General Overseer of the church was a man of God. However, since the man had relocated with his family to Canada for personal reasons, they were concerned about the newly appointed pastor, Andrew, based on some things they heard about him.

Despite her parents' worries, Adesua liked the church and had no intention of leaving anytime soon, especially now that she was an executive member of the church's Singles Fellowship. The Fellowship's executive team originally consisted of four members, but last year, Pastor Andrew expanded it by adding Adesua and three others.

About a year and a half ago, Andrew was appointed the pastor after the senior pastor relocated. Shortly after, he initiated several changes to the church's structure. One significant change was reducing the mid-week service from twice a week to once a week, on Thursdays, citing the busy schedules of the congregation, most of whom were professionals and business people. Additionally, he appointed a new music director to enhance the church's worship music, though some members questioned the director's spiritual depth.

Andrew also included Adesua and the other three people in the Singles Fellowship's executive team, to elevate the status of the church.

When Adesua joined the church three years ago, she was expected to complete a one-month Membership Class before joining any department. However, she claimed to be too busy to attend. At that time, the General Overseer was still around, and he made it clear that she wouldn't be allowed to serve without completing the class.

The new pastor, Andrew, however, saw things differently. He believed that Adesua didn't need to go through the Class, after all, she was not a young believer. He told the minister in charge of the Singles Fellowship that even though Adesua was relatively new in the church, she was a mature Christian who could quote Scriptures and preach.

That was how Adesua became an executive member of the Fellowship despite not having regularly attended church services. Since her appointment, she had been actively supporting the Fellowship financially and making an effort to attend its events. She had also preached at the Singles Fellowship, which met bi-monthly.

Adesua and her friends started praying together every Monday at 9pm since five months ago, in May, after her breakup with Jimi. They chose to pray because they realized their church didn't emphasize prayer much.

At that time, Jimi was still attending the same church, *God's Word Assembly*. Adesua liked the fact that he was a church member, had a good job, and a car; three things that were very important to her.

What she did not like was that she was taller than him.

When she realized that Jimi had likely developed feelings for her and might soon express his interest, she discussed her concern with her friends, Nancy and Moyo.

"I don't think I'd want to marry a short man. Jimi can't be more than five feet five inches. I'm five-eleven; that's like six inches taller!"

Nancy laughed. "That's not much."

"At least six inches taller without shoes. With shoes, especially high ones, I'll be a head taller!" Adesua added.

"So what?! Is it a bad thing if you're taller than your man?" Moyo asked.

"Don't miss my point. I'm not saying it's bad." Adesua answered. "My point is that if I marry such a man, high heels would be out of it for me, and you know how much I love to wear shoes with high heels." Shaking her head, she added, "That's a deal breaker for me."

Her friends tried to convince her that height should not be a big deal, and she could still wear high heels if she married a man who was shorter, but she didn't agree.

When Jimi revealed his feelings to her, she revealed her concern to him—she was taller than him. He wasn't bothered though. He laughed and encouraged her to pray to know the will of God. He didn't believe that height should be a deal breaker, a sentiment her mother also shared when Adesua brought it up with her.

Adesua didn't pray much about it, however; she still wanted what she desired.

She later on changed her mind. Considering Jimi's love for her, his many admirable qualities, and her friends' encouragement, she ultimately decided to marry him.

They began to go steady even though she couldn't say that she loved him, or he was God's will for her. They also chose not to inform Pastor Andrew, for two reasons: Jimi disagreed with some of the new pastor's decisions, while Adesua felt she didn't need to involve him in her personal matters.

The relationship eventually collapsed, regardless. (**Read: Friends to Forever**)

Whenever Adesua remembered Jimi, she wondered if she should have stayed in the relationship. If she had, she likely would be married by now.

One thing she did not wonder about was the way she treated Jimi. She knew it wasn't right. She had dragged him into an on-and-off relationship, something she never expected or wanted. It happened because she couldn't make up her mind. Convinced she deserved a better man, she believed she could find one. Proud of her flawless skin, height, American accent, and early career success, she felt she had class. With her parents' achievements as a backdrop, she told herself she wouldn't settle for a man who lacked any of the things she desired in a husband.

Besides, she wanted to be a model at a time but changed her mind when she became a Christian at the age of eighteen. She was no longer pursuing that, but she should be able to marry a man who looked like one. She wouldn't want a situation where she would be stuck with Jimi.

She grew up hearing people tell her that she was beautiful. It didn't mean much to her when she was very young. In elementary school in the US, she paid no attention to it, but as she grew older, she came to appreciate it because boys admired her, and girls wanted to be her friend. However, she didn't let it get into her head a lot, as her mother had always told her and her sisters that outer beauty would fade, and inner beauty was what truly mattered.

This kept Adesua in line. She focused on her education, pursued her passion, and was now a TV presenter.

She usually discussed her concerns with her mother, and trusted her counsel, except about men and fashion. She thought her mother was old school. Adesua would like to make her own decisions in those areas.

And so, Adesua said *yes* to Jimi in December, broke up with him in February, reconciled with him some days after and broke up with him again in March. They reconciled again, but when she met a man whom she liked, she broke up with him again in May.

When the relationship ended this time, Jimi, who had been having doubts about Pastor Andrew, stopped attending the church altogether.

As it turned out, the man that Adesua left Jimi for, disappointed her. She had met the widowed businessman through a client. At first, he seemed like the right man. He was a Christian and rich. Before long, she discovered that he was also very jealous. He complained that she sometimes closed late at work, didn't have much time for him, was usually in company of men, and too independent for his liking. He obviously didn't trust her, and she began to feel like he was suffocating her.

She was respected in her profession, but it seemed that the man was trying to reduce her to nothing. This hurt her, and she had to quickly end the relationship before the man could end her career and turn her into another person.

Afterward, she decided to send a message to Jimi. In it, she apologized for ending their relationship and made it clear that she'd like to see him so they could discuss it.

He replied.

It's over, Adesua, but we can remain friends.

Apparently, he had had enough of their toxic relationship.

She checked his Instagram page later and discovered that he had started worshipping at *The Believers Church*, the church where his female childhood friend, Rachel, worshipped.

She and Jimi hadn't talked since then.

At the time Adesua was in a relationship with Jimi, Nancy and Moyo were still very much single. Now, Moyo was in a relationship and planning to marry next year. Nancy had also met a man she hoped to marry.

And last month, Adesua's immediate younger sister, Efua, announced that she had found her ideal man as well. When she brought him home, Adesua was surprised to find Efua was taller than him. Adesua recalled how, when she told her siblings she was taller than Jimi, Efua had laughed and insisted she wouldn't date anyone shorter. Yet here she was, in love with a man who didn't meet that height requirement. Well, Adesua couldn't say her sister had misled her; leaving Jimi was her choice.

Now, with her friends and sister in serious relationships, Adesua was starting to feel desperate. While she knew younger siblings sometimes marry before their elders, she didn't want that to happen in her case. Deep down, she hoped to get married before her sisters. But where was her husband?

She couldn't understand why she was still single. *Lord, what's going on?!* It baffled her, especially since she had a good job, was beautiful with a great smile, was intelligent, and had been a Christian for some years.

CHAPTER 3

ADESUA AND HER friends' prayers ended around 9.30pm, and then they began to converse.

She got up from her bed and with the phone pressed to her left ear with her left hand, she left the room. She headed straight to the kitchen to grab some food, soon returning to her room with a plate in her right hand. She didn't get any water since she already had two bottles waiting for her in the room.

She blessed her food and as she began to eat, her eyes bounced around her room. Her bed featured a lovely headboard and three coordinating pillows. An elegant bedside lamp cast a warm glow at night when the main light was off. The walls displayed three framed photographs and a tasteful piece of art. The room also boasted a large built-in closet, elegant curtains, and a plush rug on the floor, among other charming details. Some books and magazines were on her bedside table.

She and her friends talked about their day, and then her friends began to talk about the men in their lives.

Then Nancy asked Adesua, "That reminds me, how's Jimi doing? Any news about him?"

Adesua laughed. "None, but I guess he's doing well. As the saying goes… no news is good news."

"I must confess that I was surprised when he left the church." Nancy added.

"Well, it wasn't very surprising to me. He wasn't too pleased with some of the changes at the church since the senior pastor relocated." Adesua revealed. "I guess what happened between us was the last straw that broke the camel's back."

They laughed.

"I'll send him a message on WhatsApp now. I'm sure he'll be surprised to hear from me," Adesua said with a chuckle.

As she typed Jimi's name in the search bar, she wondered if they could still reconnect. She doubted he was in another relationship yet.

His account appeared in the search results, and she examined his profile picture, which featured a man and a woman. Their gazes suggested they were a couple. The man resembled Jimi, but the small size of the image made it hard to be certain. Could it be him? If so, who was the woman? Had he already found someone else?

She clicked on the picture to enlarge it and what she saw shocked her.

"What?!" She exclaimed.

"What's that?" Her friends asked.

"Jimi and Rachel?!"

"Jimi and Rachel? Who is Rachel?" Moyo wanted to know.

"I hope it's not what I'm thinking," she remarked.

She checked the profile status and saw … *Pleasant surprises! Thank You Lord!*

"It's a lie!" She announced.

"What's that?" Her friends repeated. "What's happening? Are you okay?"

"Check Jimi's profile picture on WhatsApp!" She told them.

Her friends had his number, and before long, they were seeing what Adesua was seeing.

"Who is the lady?" Nancy asked.

"That's the lady I told you about, the one he claimed was just a friend!"

When Adesua was with Jimi, she had mentioned to her friends that he had a close female friend.

"That friend?!" Moyo said.

"Yes!" She confirmed.

"Wow!" Nancy exclaimed.

"Well, you're no longer in a relationship with him. He's free to move on." Moyo pointed out.

"It sure didn't take him long to move on though." Nancy added.

"He can move on, but … Rachel?! He told me there was nothing between them!" Adesua complained.

Looking at the picture made her grow hot with anger. She began to type.

You told me you and Rachel were just friends! You lied to me! 👻

With a click, it was sent. The blue check mark appeared beside her message almost immediately, indicating that Jimi had read it.

"I've sent a message to him." She informed her friends.

And almost immediately, WhatsApp indicated that Jimi was typing. *Good.* Adesua had more to say, but she decided to wait for his response first before giving him a piece of her mind.

As she continued talking with her friends, she kept a close watch on WhatsApp. Jimi was still typing. *No problem,* she would wait.

Her friends were still looking at the picture and analyzing it.

"Rachel seems to be taller than Jimi." Moyo observed.

"Yes, she is." Adesua confirmed.

"The height difference was a big issue to you, Adesua." Moyo reminded her.

"Has he responded to your message?" Nancy asked.

Adesua checked her phone and noticed that Jimi had stopped typing, leaving no message from him.

"No, not yet." She answered. "But he will." He would reply her shortly, she was sure.

When her phone alerted her of a message a minute after, she was certain it would be him, but it wasn't. It was a sound engineer at the TV station.

And twenty minutes after she said goodnight to her friends, there was still no reply from Jimi.

Later, as she climbed into her queen-sized bed at 11pm, she checked her phone again and was surprised to find he still hadn't responded. Jimi was usually the type to clarify things and explain himself. She knew he had seen her message, so why wasn't he replying?

Putting the phone down, she prayed briefly, and then began to think about her life.

Shortly after, her mind went to Rachel. When she was still in a relationship with Jimi, she had asked him about Rachel, and she could still remember their conversation that day.

He laughed and explained, "We are close because we grew up together, but I assure you that there's nothing between us. We're just friends."

She was silent for some seconds, and then she spoke again. "I've met her three times now. The first time was when we went to her house and then we met at two of your friends' events. She was pleasant but -" She paused for a moment before adding, "but I couldn't shake off the feeling that there was something going on. I was able to pick some vibes from her."

"What vibes?" He had asked.

"That she likes you. I'm not sure. I can't quite put my finger on it, but it feels like something's there."

"It might just be your imagination," he replied.

"Are you sure?"

He glanced at her briefly. "You should know some things about me by now. I don't tell lies, and I won't cheat on you. There's nothing between Rachel and me." He assured her.

She believed him. He was the kind of man who didn't play games; he was sincere. Besides, he had known Rachel long before he met her, and if he had wanted to marry Rachel, he wouldn't have needed to propose to her, Adesua had reasoned that day.

Now, it appeared that things had changed between Jimi and Rachel, and this confirmed her intuition about Rachel; Rachel loved Jimi.

Does Jimi love Rachel? When exactly did things change between them? Adesua couldn't help wondering, upset.

But why am I upset that he has moved on? She asked herself, after all, she didn't love him then, and she didn't love him now.

As she considered it, she realized her bruised ego was at the heart of the matter. She felt hurt because he had moved on. She had expected him to wait until she could make up her mind. She would have preferred he remained alone and lonely, or better yet, that he had come to her, and begged to make their relationship work.

She knew she hadn't treated him well and that she was to blame for their breakup. Yet it still hurt to see him move on, especially with Rachel.

Adesua dragged her mind to her job. She would be interviewing a woman on Friday, and she had planned to prepare some interview questions this evening before sleeping. With the way things were, however, she wouldn't be able to do so as she was not in the right frame of mind. It would be best to get some sleep now. She should have a clear mind in the morning to prepare the questions. But as she closed her eyes, her thoughts lingered on Rachel and Jimi, and she drifted off still contemplating them.

Her alarm went off at 7am as it did everyday except Saturday and public holidays when she slept in. Opening one eye, she reached out a hand and stopped it.

As she let herself slowly wake up, she found that she still had Jimi and Rachel on her mind, but she was no longer greatly bothered. With a sigh, she rolled out of bed to use the bathroom, and then returned to bed.

She had a busy day ahead and she pushed thoughts about Jimi and Rachel aside so she could get some things done before finally getting up from bed.

Every morning when she woke up, she prayed, after which she checked her e-mail, WhatsApp, and other social media accounts. She would then reply important messages and post whatever she needed to post on her social media accounts. Being on social media was part of her job.

Now, as she started with the rituals of her day, she could hear her parents' voices and movements in the living room. Her sisters usually left the house earlier.

Knowing her father must be preparing to go to his office, she stopped what she was doing, brought her long legs from the bed, and got up. Putting her feet on the floor, she slid them into her white flip-flops and left the room.

Her father was at the breakfast table while her mother was in the kitchen. She greeted them and then returned to her room to continue what she was doing.

As it was the first day of November, she composed a new month greeting and began forwarding it to several people in her contacts.

Before long, she heard the opening and closing of the house's front door. Shortly after, her mother came to inform her that breakfast was on the table for her, and she thanked her.

Adesua eventually left bed around 9.30am and navigated to the bathroom for a quick shower.

Breakfast was boiled yam, fish sauce, one boiled egg, and chocolate tea. It didn't take her long to devour everything, and back in her room, she sat at her desk and began to prepare the questions for the interview.

She eventually left the house at noon, carrying a small box that contained two of her clothes. She would be having a photoshoot today at the TV station. That would take some time, after which she would meet with her production team to discuss her next show and organize schedules. She would also be having a meeting with someone at a restaurant around 6pm.

She returned home around 8.30pm, and by now, it was clear that Jimi did not intend to reply her.

The house was dark and empty; no one was around. Since it was Tuesday, she knew her parents were likely at church for prayer service. Her sisters might still be at work or could have gone to church as well.

She turned on the light in the living room and strode into her room. There, she set the small box she had taken out with her on a side. Removing her clothes, she folded them and put them in the laundry bag in a corner of the room. She wore casual dress and went to the kitchen to get something to eat. Back in her room, she showered, wore her nightdress, and sat cross-legged in bed, to use her phone.

CHAPTER 4

FOUR DAYS AFTER, on Saturday, Jimi had not replied, and Adesua found it difficult to believe that he had chosen to ignore her.

In the afternoon, she decided to contact him again as she still had things she'd like to say to him. Scrolling down to his name, she saw that the profile picture was still the same.

She sent him a message and kept checking to see if he had read it, but only one checkmark appeared. Clicking on his information, she found that his status was not showing. She went on Instagram and found they were no longer friends. It was the same on Facebook and other platforms. He had unfriended her on social media. Could he have blocked her on WhatsApp? She wondered. Finding it difficult to believe, she tried to call him, but it didn't go through. Yes, he had blocked her.

Hmm, Jimi had definitely burned the bridge and moved on. Feeling terribly upset, she told herself that it would not have hurt so much if she were in a relationship.

She prayed, "God, give me my husband. I'm turning twenty eight next Saturday!"

In the morning of the next day, Sunday, she got dressed for church, had a quick bowl of cereal, and headed out. There was traffic on the way, and by the time she got to church, the praise and worship session had already begun. After parking her car and grabbing her handbag which contained her Bible, iPad, iPhone, and wallet, she alighted from the car and walked toward the hall. Clad in a simple floral dress, complemented by her high heels and jewelry, she looked effortlessly elegant as always.

The hall's glass door which had a wooden frame was pulled open from inside by a uniformed female usher, and Adesua stepped inside. The air-conditioned hall with burgundy colored rug had burgundy-colored upholstered chairs. The back and the seat of the chairs were generously padded. A pouch was on the back of each chair to keep bibles and notebooks while a rack was under the seat to allow everyone to store their personal belongings.

The usher greeted Adesua nicely and led her to a row in the middle aisle. There was no one there yet, and Adesua stopped by the first seat. She put her handbag on the rack under the seat in front of her as it was empty and remained standing to join the congregation to sing. Very quickly, more people arrived, and in no time, the chair beside hers was the only empty chair left in the row.

The session ended, and as they sat down, the same female usher appeared from behind Adesua. A man was with her and she pointed at the row.

Adesua looked at the tall man as he thanked the usher.

He then looked at Adesua, and as their eyes met, he said *hi* to her. She responded and moved out of the way so he could get to the empty chair. He did and settled in.

She glanced briefly at the man again as she didn't think she had seen him in church before. When she saw his eyes flitting around, taking in his surroundings and the drapes across the high ceiling of the hall, she guessed she must be right.

As if the man sensed her looking at him, his gaze turned and settled on hers before she could look away. A corner of his mouth turned up in a subtle smile. "This is a beautiful church."

She nodded and returned the smile. Who was he? She wondered, curious, before returning her gaze to the front of the church.

When it was time for announcement, the announcer mentioned some of the church's activities, and then said that the singles would be having an event in December.

Then the man called Adesua. "Could you please come to give us more details about the event?"

She stood and as she walked to the front, she felt a twinge of self-consciousness. In front, she collected the microphone and with a smile, started, "Good morning, Church!"

Without wasting time, she gave the details of the event, including the activities lined up, inspiring talks, and the name of the guest speaker. The event would hold on Saturday, the third day of December, at 6pm, in the church hall.

Then she announced, "It's going to be a wonderful opportunity for fellowship and fun, and to connect with one another. Of course, there will be food, so just come to enjoy yourself. I hope to see all the singles in the house there. If anyone needs more information, feel free to contact me or any of the executives."

She gave the microphone back to the announcer and returned to her seat.

The announcement continued, and as she sat down, the man beside her looked at her and smiled. "Adesua! Wow! Before you were called out, I had the feeling that I'd seen you somewhere before, but I couldn't place it."

She smiled. People usually told her "I know you. I see you on TV."

He added, "It's nice to meet you."

She responded, still smiling.

He spoke again. "I'm new in the church … today's my second time."

"Oh, great!"

"So, you're one of the singles executives?"

She nodded. "Yes."

"Awesome! Well, I hope to attend the event. It will be a busy day for me, but I'll do my best to be there."

Her eyelids were raised to show surprise. "You're single?!" *He's single?!*

He smiled and shrugged. "Yes, I am. I may not be able to attend the singles' services regularly though, because of my other commitments."

"I understand."

"I'll talk to you about it after the service." He promised.

"Alright." She looked forward to that.

When the service finally ended, everyone rose to leave.

The man asked her, "Can I talk to you now?"

"Sure."

They walked to a side of the church, near a door.

She faced him and had a good look at him. He was handsome, assured, and alert. She could see that he was taller than her, by about two inches. He would also be older than her; around thirty five, by her guess.

"My name is Tony." He began.

"It's nice to meet you."

He chuckled. "The pleasure is mine, trust me. I watch your show on TV."

"Thank you."

His eyes went to her elegant handbag and noticing the Dior label, he remarked, "That's a nice bag."

She appreciated him, and then he went on. "I'm new here and would like to participate in the activities as much as possible. I'd like you to keep me informed if that's okay by you."

"Sure."

"Great. Regarding the upcoming event, I'd like to contribute financially."

He mentioned an amount. It wasn't much, but she thanked him.

He added, "I'd have loved to do more but I'm involved in some projects presently."

Reaching inside his jacket, he produced a card. "Here's my card." He said with a smile as he handed it to her. "Could I get your number?" He asked, pulling out his phone.

She glanced at the phone and immediately recognized it as an expensive model, similar to her own. *Impressive—he must have a great job.*

"I can give you my card." She said. Opening her handbag, she brought out a small stack of beautifully printed cards and took one.

As she handed it to him, his fingers brushed against hers briefly.

Looking at her card, he read her name and contact details that were printed on the front side of the beautiful card. "Adesua Okalo, The Adesua Show, JKITV." He called slowly, as if test running it.

They talked a little more and then it was time to say goodbye.

"I'll stay in touch." He promised.

She hoped he would.

As he walked away, she looked at him. He was well dressed and looked polished. *Hmm.*

She eventually got home around 3pm and found her parents at the lunch table. She greeted them and then went to her room to change her clothes. When she returned to the living room, she joined them at the table. She asked after her sisters and was told that they hadn't returned from church.

After lunch, she sat in the living room with her parents, to relax and talk.

Her father was an example of a family man. If he wasn't busy with his law practice, he would be in church, or at home with his family. Not a party person, he was happy spending a quiet weekend with his family.

In her room later, Adesua brought out Tony's card and as she saved his name and number on her phone, she smiled. He was her kind of man. If he was still available, she'd like to get to know him better.

Afterward, she called the head of the Singles Fellowship to tell him that Tony would like to be involved in the fellowship. Also, with her birthday coming up next Saturday, she invited the man to her house, where she'd be hosting a few friends to celebrate.

When the call ended, she decided to rest for a while, knowing she had an event to attend that evening. At the right time, she got up and began getting ready for the outing.

On Saturday, her birthday, she woke up feeling excited and special. She prayed and then began to check some of the many congratulatory messages on her phone, smiling. She just loved the influx of messages and calls wishing her a happy birthday. Some of them were from people she seldom talked with. She also looked forward to the presents she would receive from some people later in the day. Her parents and siblings had already given her presents.

The day went well for her. She celebrated the special occasion by hosting her friends, family, and the church members who came to her house to rejoice with her.

During church service the next day, Sunday, she glanced around to catch a glimpse of Tony, but didn't see him.

When it was time to testify of God's goodness, she got up and went to the front, to join the six people who were already standing there. Some minutes after, it was her turn, and she announced that she was grateful to God for yet another birthday yesterday.

The church service ended about two hours after, and she carried her handbag. As she made her way to the exit, she saw Tony approaching her, and she smiled, happy to see him.

He reached her and with a broad smile began to sing, "Happy Birthday to you, all glory to God, long life is your portion, Happy Birthday to you."

This meant he was in church when she was giving her testimony, she thought.

"Aww." She giggled and put her right hand over her chest to show appreciation. "Thank you."

He congratulated her and prayed briefly.

"Amen." She responded. "It's good to see you again."

"Same here."

They exchanged pleasantries briefly, and then he wanted to know how she celebrated her birthday. "Hope you had a great time."

"Yes, I did." She answered and went on to tell him that she celebrated with a small gathering of her friends and family.

Then she said, "I'd like to introduce you to the head of the Singles Fellowship, if you don't mind."

"That would be great."

She led Tony to the man and introduced them. She also introduced him to Nancy and Moyo.

When she was talking to Nancy and Moyo later in the evening, they wanted to know more about Tony, and she told them the little she knew about him.

The following Sunday, Tony was one of the people who went forward to give a testimony. He revealed he had just relocated to the city; he was a minister in his former church and the members were sorry to see him leave. He said he would like to thank God for bringing him to this church. Some of his friends wanted him to join their church because they knew he was a crowd puller and would be an asset to their church. However, four Sundays ago, he got in his car and began to drive around, looking for a church to worship, and saw this church.

As he talked, Adesua listened, impressed. She believed he would be an asset to the church, and the church would have to find ways to make him stay. She wondered if Pastor

Andrew and the head of the men's group were seeing what she was seeing.

Tony continued talking, and then he said, "This church is awesome! I'm still single, and somehow, I have a feeling that my wife is in this church."

Some people laughed while others clapped, excited.

Adesua smiled. Well, if Tony had a feeling his future wife was in this church, she could say she had a feeling that Tony liked her. And, if she was honest with herself, she guessed she liked him too. He was the kind of man she'd like to be seen with and marry. Could he be the one for her?

And why was he still single at his age … a man with his looks and confidence, who claimed to be a crowd puller and an asset? She wondered.

CHAPTER 5

ADESUA DECIDED TO look for Tony after service to greet him. However, before she could look for him when the service ended, she saw him coming in her direction, beaming at her.

"That was a powerful testimony." She said when he reached her.

"Thank you. I needed to say it. The Lord has been good to me. I'll tell you more about it. Let me take you out to lunch to celebrate your birthday." He told her, still smiling.

Oh, wow! She'd love that but … she had just met him. She hesitated, and then replied, "I'm not sure, but I appreciate the offer. Thank you."

"Why? Is it because we've only just met?"

"Well, yes." She admitted.

He chuckled. "Well, what better way to get to know me than over lunch? We could head to the restaurant down the street. I was there last week, and it's pretty decent."

She had been to the restaurant twice, and she knew it was okay. She would prefer one of the best rated restaurants in town, but since she had just met him, the restaurant down the street would serve.

He spoke again. "I'll introduce myself properly to you over lunch. What do you say?"

She agreed.

"Great!" He smiled, pleased with himself. "How do we move? Would you like us to walk down to the place or go in my car?"

She said she would prefer they go in their separate cars, so that she could go home from there, and he agreed.

She told her friends she was going to the restaurant with him.

****

Tony and Adesua walked to the parking lot together, and he escorted her to her car before heading to his, which was closer to the gate. He arrived at the restaurant ahead of her, parked, and stepped out of his car. His phone was in his hand, and he opened it to check his messages.

He was still on the phone when he noticed a sleek car pull up. The driver was a woman, and as she got closer, he realized it was Adesua.

This is her car?! Wow! In that moment, he made up his mind to do whatever it took to marry her. She was the kind of woman he needed in his life.

Smiling, he waited for her to park, and then he went over. "This is a nice car." He told her.

"Thank you."

She exited the car and locked up. "Where are you parked?" She asked. She'd like to know the kind of car he had.

He pointed. "That's my car."

It's not bad, she thought.

"I plan to buy another car soon." He stated.

As they walked side by side toward the entrance, he continued talking about cars.

At the door, he stepped ahead and pulled the door open. She thanked him graciously as she passed him.

He followed her. A waiter welcomed them and as he led them to a table for two, Adesua's pointed heel shoes made a soft clicking sound on the marble floor.

The waiter took their order, and the moment he left, Tony resumed his discussion about cars.

"My next car will be a Nissan Murano SV." He announced and began to tell her what he liked about it.

They were still talking about it when the waiter brought their drinks.

When the waiter left, he began to talk about himself. He lived in Warri, before relocating.

He was a big sports fan, and when he mentioned he was a Man U supporter, she laughed and shared that she liked Chelsea. This sparked a conversation about sports that lasted for several minutes.

He told her he was a university graduate, an engineer turned businessman, and he was doing well.

He added, "There's a big contract I'm pursuing, and I believe it will go through before long. Please remember me in your prayers."

Without asking what the business was about, she prayed, "The Lord will do it in Jesus' name."

He said a loud Amen.

Then he went on to say that he was friends with some big pastors. "Pastor Jonathan Mebude knows me very well. I'm sure you know who that is, right?"

"Yes."

"I'll show you some pictures so you can know it's not a joke." He took his phone and opened the photo gallery. "Here."

He turned his phone to her so she could see a picture. It was that of him and Pastor Jonathan. They were standing with two other men.

He began to show her pictures of him with some pastors and celebrities, including comedians, and actors.

"And this is my picture with the deputy governor." He mentioned the name of the state.

****

As Adesua listened to Tony and looked at the pictures on his phone, she had a feeling that some of the things he was saying weren't true. He was definitely a smooth talker, and she encountered his type regularly in her line of work. People like him have charisma and use their charm to manipulate or persuade others into believing their lies. But she kept her opinions to herself.

Before long, the waiter brought their food, and as they began to eat, they began to talk about *God's Word Assembly*. He told her he liked the church and liked the fact that the midweek service held just once. He wasn't fond of churches that held lengthy services.

She told him she shared his opinion.

He made her know that he mentored young men and women in his former church and would like an opportunity to teach in the Singles Fellowship one of these days.

"That would be awesome!" She commented.

He wanted to know more about her work as a TV presenter, and she told him.

When they were ready to leave, the bill was brought, and he settled it promptly.

Outside, he told her, "Let's stay in touch."

"Definitely." She agreed.

On her way home, Adesua was smiling. Even though she sensed that Tony wasn't entirely truthful and tended to exaggerate, she still had a good time. He was witty, funny, and smart. He also seemed to know a lot about everything … politics, cars, business, sports, church, relationships. And he looked like he could seamlessly fit into any environment … a casual gathering or a formal dinner.

At home, she called her friends, and as she told them about the outing with Tony, they had a good laugh. She told them what she thought of him; he was a smooth talker, for sure.

Still, she couldn't get him out of her mind.

In the evening, she was in the kitchen cutting up two oranges to eat as a snack when her phone began to ring. She was surprised but happy when Tony's name appeared on the screen. He apparently had been thinking of her as she had been thinking of him.

She quickly answered it. "Hi, Tony."

"Adesua, hi."

"I was just going to call you." She said, and then thanked him again for the birthday lunch.

"The pleasure was all mine, trust me. Lunch … with Adesua for company?! It made my day!"

She giggled, her eyes sparkling with enthusiasm.

As they chatted, he casually asked when she'd be in the studio the following week. She paused for a moment, considering, and then, deciding it was fine to share, she told him her schedule.

That week, on Tuesday, she was in the studio preparing for her show when she was told that Tony was there to see her.

She called his phone. "You're here?!"

"Yes." He said and laughed.

"Wow!" She was surprised and delighted. "I'm coming."

When she got to the reception, he greeted her with a bright smile and gave her a hug. "How's my favorite TV presenter doing today?"

She giggled. "She's doing well. This is a surprise. What brings you here?"

He said he knew he would be coming to the area, and that was why he asked her on Sunday when she would be in the studio so he could surprise her.

He went on. "I wanted to stop by to say hello to my favorite TV presenter and have a glimpse of some of the behind the scenes activities."

She giggled again. "Thank you. You just made my day. Come on in."

As she led him to her office, he said he knew she would be busy, as such, he would not stay long.

"Thanks for coming." She responded.

In her office, she introduced him to the people there, and then offered him something to drink.

He wanted to know the account he would transfer the money he promised to give the Singles Fellowship into, and she gave it to him. He pressed some buttons on his phone, and within a minute, he said it was done.

Adesua thanked him and said she would let the person in charge know. She hadn't expected that he would actually give the money; she had assumed it was just an empty promise. Now that he had kept his word, she felt that her judgment of his character might have been mistaken.

She was curious whether he would attend the Singles event on Saturday, and he confirmed he would be there. When he asked if he could bring a friend or two, she agreed.

Soon, he was ready to leave. As she saw him off to the reception, he took her hand and said, "I hope I didn't take too much of your time."

Smiling, she looked down at their joined hands before looking at him. "No, I'm glad you came."

At the reception, she said goodbye. "I'll see you on Saturday."

In the evening, she called him to appreciate him again for visiting her at the studio.

"It was nice seeing you there. It's obvious that you love what you do." He said.

"Oh yeah, I do."

"That's how it's supposed to be. I'm happy for you and proud of you." He told her.

"Thank you."

"I know you're very busy, but I hope we can go somewhere for dinner one of these days."

"That would be great." She responded. "I'd like to pay this time, though."

"Oh no, don't worry, it's my treat." He said.

He called her twice that week.

And on Saturday, she saw him at the Singles event which went well. He moved around, took pictures, and chatted with others as if he was one of the executive members.

On Sunday, after the church service, they met, and he told her he and the friend he invited had a good time.

That week, they chatted on WhatsApp everyday and talked on phone thrice. On Thursday evening, they were in church for Carol service and sat together.

As they spent time together, her opinion of him that he was not a straightforward person seemed to fade away. She didn't think it mattered much. What mattered was that he liked her and was pursuing her. What if he exaggerated and said some things that were untrue? It simply showed that he had a weakness and was not perfect, she reasoned. She told herself that no one was perfect, including her, and she shouldn't expect perfection from Tony. Besides, there was no one that God could not change, and she believed that Tony would change, given time.

She also started telling Moyo and Nancy positive things about Tony; to change the impression she had previously given them of him being a smooth talker. She wanted them to accept him as a friend.

Adesua and Tony saw each other in church on Sunday morning, and in the evening, they went to a restaurant for dinner.

As they ate, they talked and laughed.

She wanted to know his age and he said he was thirty six.

She knew she was supposed to reveal her own age, but she didn't.

He wasn't offended anyway, he simply said, "Don't tell me yours yet, let me guess." He stared at her for some seconds and then said, "You're in your late twenties. Is that correct?"

She nodded.

"Twenty … eight?"

"Yes."

He clapped and chuckled, looking pleased with himself. He added, "And I know that your birthday is November 12. I've taken note of that."

She giggled again. "When is yours?"

"July 30."

"Noted."

She wanted to know about his family, and he said everyone was in Warri. When she told him about her own family, he said he looked forward to meeting them.

He told her he lived in a one-bedroom apartment, but he planned to move into a bigger apartment soon.

Before they left the restaurant, she invited him to an event she had to attend on Friday evening, and he accepted. He offered to pick her up at home for the event, and she gave him her house address.

On their way out of the restaurant, she wondered what the future had in store for them. She hoped that this was the beginning of something great between them.

She would be getting Christmas gifts for families and friends the next day, Monday. When it occurred to her that she would need to give Tony a gift, she began to think of a good gift.

On Monday afternoon, she went to some stores. She got the gifts she wanted, and at home, she wrapped them.

That Friday, he arrived on time, at 5pm, and sat in the living room, to wait for her. Glancing around, he liked everything he saw. *Adesua's parents are rich,* and he told himself he must marry her.

Adesua didn't take long, and soon, they were on their way out. She was holding a gift bag, and inside his car, she presented it to him. "Have a Merry Christmas."

"Oh, you beat me to it." He lied. "I already got a gift for you, but I had thought that I'd give it to you later."

"No problem." She believed him.

They had a wonderful time at the event, and he brought her home around 10pm.

On Tuesday, she chose to attend a colleague's birthday celebration and arrived around 6pm. As she entered, she spotted a friend and paused to greet her.

While they exchanged pleasantries, her gaze wandered, and she was surprised to see Tony. She felt happy at the sight, but she noticed he wasn't alone; two men and two women were with him. One of the women was seated next to Tony, and Adesua wondered who she was.

She made her way over, but just before reaching him, she noticed the bottles in front of Tony were beer bottles—a surprising detail.

Tony was just as surprised to see her. He stood up to greet her warmly and invited her to join their table, but she politely declined and headed to another table instead. She caught sight of him saying something to his friends before he left his table to join her.

He explained that a friend had invited him to the ceremony. "I didn't know I'd see you here," he said.

"Obviously," she replied, feeling a wave of disappointment. She was curious about the woman next to him but didn't want to ask; after all, they weren't in a relationship.

It was as if he could sense her thoughts when he added, "The ladies are just friends of those guys."

"Well, what I saw suggested otherwise. The woman beside you seemed like a close friend of yours." She countered.

He laughed and shook his head. "She's just friendly with me, that's all. You know how I am; I like to chat with everyone."

She decided to let it go and asked, "So, you drink alcohol?"

He sighed and admitted it was a weakness he hadn't conquered yet, asking her to pray for him.

She took a deep breath. *Another weakness*?!

A server was passing by their table and Tony stopped him. "What kind of food is available? This person has just arrived."

Adesua shook her head to decline. "No, thanks. I'll be leaving shortly."

Tony tried to press her to take something, but she said no, and the server left. She explained to Tony that she seldom ate at such events.

When she was ready to leave, he said he would leave as well. He went to say goodbye to his friends and then returned to Adesua's table, and together they left the venue. This made her happy. He cared for her, after all, she thought, and she decided to overlook his weaknesses.

On Christmas Day, she saw him at church, where he presented her with a gift. Later that afternoon, he came to her house to pick her up, and they went out together. As they talked during the drive, they agreed to go to the beach on Saturday, the last day of the year, before meeting again in the evening for the crossover service at church.

That Saturday, Tony arrived at her house around 9am, and they headed out to the beach.

There, while strolling around, they came across a spot selling food and drinks. They stopped, bought what they wanted, and left. They had to pay to sit under a bamboo shed with picnic chairs, and they decided to do so.

When they finished eating, he mentioned that he had something to tell her.

"Go ahead, I'm listening."

"You know, I've been thinking a lot about you, us. You're special." He began.

Adesua was smiling as she looked at him.

He continued. "You know, the day we first met, I had a feeling you'd be someone special to me. Two Sundays later, when I was giving my testimony, I mentioned that I felt my future wife was in the church ... I'm not sure if you heard me say it that day."

She nodded. "Yes, I did."

He took her hand. "I think God brought us together. I care about you, and I'd want you to pray about me, about a future together with me in marriage."

"Wow!" She exclaimed.

"Yes, Wow!"

"I wasn't expecting this now."

He chuckled. "I didn't want the year to end without you knowing how I feel about you."

"I appreciate that, but ... we met not too long ago." She said.

He laughed. "I know, but how long does it take to know someone or to know that you care about someone?"

She inhaled deeply.

"You care about me; you have feelings for me, don't you?"

"Yes." She admitted.

"You see, if you know you know." He declared, smiling broadly.

She giggled.

"If there's anything you'd like to know about me, ask and I'll answer you as best as I can."

She giggled again, and then asked him some questions which he answered. He also had some questions for her.

Afterward, he said, "Tell me you'll consider my proposal."

"I definitely will." She promised, happy.

Taking a deep breath, he added, "I'd like to say that at this point, I wouldn't want a long courtship period. When a person meets the right one, there's no reason to delay. Besides, at thirty six, I'd like to settle down on time."

She nodded. "I understand."

"One more thing, I'd want us to keep this to ourselves for now, until the time is right … and I'll tell you why."

She listened.

"I've been in a serious relationship twice … but we involved too many people: families, friends, and the church. Everyone seemed to have an opinion about the relationships. Things became complicated and the relationships failed. I don't want that to happen to us. Sometimes, involving people could bring confusion and complications. Of course, we will involve them, but not now."

He took her hand in a pleading way, "Let's solidify our relationship first before we tell people. I hope you understand."

She said yes and told herself that he had a point. She had told her friends and family about Jimi and other men in her life, and now, she was still single. She probably said too much. She would handle things differently this time, she decided. No one would learn about her relationship with Tony until it was absolutely necessary.

"Are we in agreement?" He wanted to know.

She nodded. "Yes, sure."

When they were ready to leave, they took some pictures together, and on their way to the parking lot, he took her hand in his.

About two hours after, they reached her house. She thanked him for a wonderful outing and exited his car.

In her room, she got in bed to rest a little before she would need to go to church, but her mind was filled with Tony and his proposal.

She began to talk to God. "Tony's a Christian, and the kind of man I want. I'm falling in love with him already … I don't want to lose him, but he still has some weaknesses." She couldn't deny the fact that some things didn't seem right in his life, and she prayed that the Lord would transform his life.

She would have loved to tell her friends and mother about this new development, but she had an agreement with Tony. Besides, if she told them about his 'weaknesses', they would discourage her, and she didn't want that.

She could make her own decision; and her decision was that she'd like to marry Tony. She wouldn't want to lose him.

Knowing she was supposed to ask God for His will, she prayed, "I'd like to marry him, but what is Your will, Lord?"

She didn't seem to hear anything, but a question came to her mind … *how well do I know Tony*? Well, he had told her a lot about himself, and she guessed she knew the important things. She would know more with time.

What about the pastor? She knew she was supposed to inform him, but she decided it would have to be later, not now.

She got up at 6pm to prepare dinner for the family, and by 10pm, she was back in church for the crossover service which ended at 12.35am. Tony was there, and he came to her to wish her a Happy New Year.

CHAPTER 6

THE FOLLOWING WEEK, Tony wanted to know if Adesua had an answer for him yet. She laughed and said not yet, but she would, before long.

The week after, they went to a recreational park, and there, she gave him the answer he wanted: yes, she would marry him.

Over the next three weeks, they saw each other regularly. Everything was going on well, and she thanked God regularly for bringing Tony into her life. He was very smart and ambitious; and he had great plans for himself which she liked.

They discussed about their future together, and he told her his business plans. He reminded her of the business he had applied for, and that she should pray along with him that it would come through quickly. He knew he would make some good profit from the business, and they would be able to get married in a grand style.

She was impressed, and she told him so. Her only concern was about his 'weaknesses'.

On the third Tuesday of February, he came to her house but didn't want to come inside, so she went out to meet him. They sat together in his car.

"I have good news!" He announced. His eyes were filled with excitement.

She smiled. "What's that?"

He said the business deal was through; he had been approved.

She was very happy. "Praise God! I'm happy for you, congratulations." She was filled with admiration.

He thanked her and went on. "The only snag is that they want me to start it with my money. And this is where you come in. I will need loan from you. I don't want to ask my friends; you know how money can destroy good friendships. I prefer to ask you since we're getting married."

This wasn't what she'd expected to hear from him. "How much are we talking about?" She asked.

"It's substantial but not so much. It's just two million naira."

"Two million naira?!" She exclaimed.

He smiled. "Yes. It's not much considering the business. In fact, it might not be enough … I'll have to find a way to manage the two million. I'll return it the moment I'm paid, I promise."

"Why don't you borrow it from a bank?"

"I've considered it, but that won't favor us. The interest will eat up the profit and that's not what we want. We would need that money for our wedding, and to live on while I pursue another business."

"Two million?!"

Smiling, he took her hand in a reassuring way. "I know what you may be thinking but don't worry, you will get your money back soon. It won't fail, I promise. I already have the job. I wouldn't have asked if I wasn't sure. As a matter of fact, I wouldn't have needed to ask you for the money if it were to be last month. I had more than enough money then and bought some parcels of land."

There was a faint warning in her mind about this, and she responded, "Well, let me think about it."

"Yes, you should think about it, but here's the thing … I have to start the project immediately." He said. "Would you be quick about it, please?"

"I understand."

"Er … one other thing please … I'm a private person. I wouldn't want you to discuss this with anyone, not even your family. It would be embarrassing to me, and I wouldn't be able to face them. I would be forced to stay away from your house. I'm doing this for us."

She said she understood.

Afterward, he wanted to know when she'd like them to get married. "I can't wait for us to get married."

They discussed and chose October.

She was both happy and concerned.

In bed that night, she lay on her back, staring up at the ceiling, her thoughts circling around the matter. Two million naira?! It was a large sum, too large not to, but stir up doubt. She sensed deceit, but quickly dismissed the idea. Why would Tony lie about this? With all the people he knew and the connections he boasted about, why would he need to deceive her?

Could it be a scam? She frowned, turning the thought over in her mind. It was possible. But Tony? No, he didn't seem like the type. Still, she reminded herself, *you can't always judge someone's heart by their appearance.* Evil could come from anyone, and anyone who didn't fear God could easily fall into wrongdoing.

That thought brought another question. *Did Tony fear the Lord?* She wasn't sure. As much as they had spent time together, it occurred to her that she didn't know him deeply. She knew the things he had told her, but beyond that, she couldn't say.

However, she loved him and they were in a relationship. *And when you love someone, you help them in their time of need,* she reasoned. She had the money, didn't she?

Still, a voice inside her pressed her to be cautious. And so, she resolved that before she gave him anything, she would get his word again. Surely, being a Christian, he would want to honor his word.

After mulling it over for what felt like hours, she decided that if she was going to help him, there was no point in dragging it out. Tomorrow, she would act.

The next morning, she sent him a message.

Will you be in church this evening?

His response came quickly.

Yes.

After the evening service, they met.

"Are you sure I will get this money back?" She began.

He laughed and assured her she would.

When she told him she was ready to give him the money, his face lit with gratitude.

"You won't regret this." He said with certainty.

She nodded, choosing to believe him. "Let me have your bank account details."

Within moments, she transferred the money, her heart thumping as she confirmed the transaction.

Two weeks passed. Everything seemed fine … until he came to her again, looking troubled. "I hate to ask, but the money you gave me … it's not enough. Could you lend me a little more?"

Her stomach knotted with concern, but she forced herself to remain calm. "How much more do you need?"

"Five hundred thousand." He said.

She hesitated as she sensed the Holy Spirit sounding alarms in her spirit. "I can only give you half of that." She finally said.

He frowned, then pressed a bit, clearly hoping for the full amount, but she stood her ground. "That's all I can spare right now."

After a moment, he nodded, conceding. "Alright, I'll manage. I'll push the company to release the funds on time."

"Please do." She replied, a slight edge to her voice. "I need my money back."

"I understand," he said with a reassuring smile. "No problem. Can I get it tomorrow?"

"I'll try."

Once again, she transferred the money.

Another week passed before she asked him about the project.

"It's going well." He assured her.

He was smiling, but something about the way he said it didn't sit right with her. His response seemed quick, almost rehearsed. When she asked if he knew when the company would pay him, he gave vague answers but assured her she would get her money soon.

Over the next three weeks, Tony said nothing about the project or the money. His focus had shifted entirely to their wedding plans, and every time they spoke, that was all he wanted to discuss. He also wanted them to get some things done before they would start informing families and friends.

"We should book the reception hall and the wedding cake soon," he said one evening, sounding eager. "The earlier we get it done, the better."

She couldn't deny that wedding planning was important, but the money weighed heavily on her mind. She had been patient, not wanting to push him too hard, but it was time to address it, she decided. "We're planning our wedding, Tony.

We need money for that. When will you get the funds from those people?"

Tony sighed and frowned as if the subject made him uncomfortable. "I don't know why it's taking so long, but you know how these things are. Delays happen."

Her anxiety deepened. "Are you sure everything is okay? I need to be certain I'll get my money back."

He flashed her a reassuring smile, his tone confident. "Of course. If there was a problem, don't you think I'd be avoiding you by now? I wouldn't keep seeing you or making all these wedding plans with you. You know that, right?"

His grin was so convincing that, despite her doubts, she found herself relaxing. What other choice did she have but to trust him anyway? She told herself that he wouldn't still be here, talking about their future together if he hadn't planned to follow through. She counseled herself to be patient.

"Alright," she said, her voice softening. "I believe you."

They went on to discuss their plans, agreeing to set aside time to check out event halls together when her schedule allowed.

She told herself that soon, everything would fall into place—the money, the wedding, and their future. But somewhere deep inside her heart, a small, persistent concern remained.

CHAPTER 7

THE FOLLOWING WEEK, Adesua received an unexpected call from Fortune, one of her close friends from university. Fortune had gotten married last year and now lived in Abuja, but the two had kept in touch. Fortune told Adesua that she was in town and staying at her uncle's house. They made plans to meet on Monday, the first day of May.

That Monday afternoon, Adesua arrived at the house and was greeted warmly by Fortune who looked radiant and happy. Adesua's eyes immediately went to the slight swell of her friend's belly. Fortune was pregnant.

"Wow! Awesome!" Adesua exclaimed, happy for her friend.

They sat together in the living room, catching up on each other's lives. Fortune talked about her marriage and life in Abuja; how different and expensive everything was in Abuja but how much she had grown to like the place. Her face glowed with excitement as she spoke about her pregnancy; the new phase she and her husband were preparing for.

After some time, Fortune leaned forward and said, "Adesua, I'm praying for you. The Lord will connect you with the right man before long, in Jesus' name."

Adesua smiled, but instead of thanking her and moving on, she decided to share her own good news. Tony wanted her to keep their relationship private for now, but she felt she could tell Fortune, after all she didn't know Tony and would be returning to Abuja the following week.

"Well," she began slowly, her eyes sparkling, "the Lord has done it."

Fortune's eyes widened. "Adesua! What do you mean?"

Adesua grinned. "I'm engaged."

Fortune's face lit up with excitement and she pulled Adesua into an embrace. "Oh, praise God!" She exclaimed. "Who is he? What's his name? Is he a member of your church?"

"Yes, he's a member of my church. His name is Tony Nnaji."

"Tony Nnaji?!" Fortune repeated, pausing for a moment, her expression thoughtful. "I know a Tony Nnaji."

"Really?" Adesua raised her eyebrows, surprised.

"Yes, but your Tony may not be the Tony I know. The one I'm talking about is tall and dark in complexion."

"This Tony is tall and dark in complexion too. Maybe it's the same person." Adesua said, a small smile tugging at the corners of her lips.

"It's possible." Fortune replied, sounding uncertain. "May I see a picture of him?"

"Sure." Adesua took out her phone and opened the photo gallery. She found a picture of Tony and handed the phone to Fortune. "Here."

As Fortune studied the picture, Adesua watched her closely. A frown emerged on Fortune's face, and then her expression shifted back to a polite smile.

"Yeah, it's Tony alright. Woah!" Fortune said with an air of surprise.

"Where did you know him from?" Adesua asked, curious.

"I knew him in Warri." Fortune answered, her tone sharp as she fell silent.

"Oh, yes, you were in Warri." Adesua remarked and nodded.

She expected Fortune to say more but when Fortune didn't elaborate, she decided to press further. "How well do you know him? What do you know about him?" She couldn't help asking.

But instead of offering more details, Fortune smiled lightly and looked away, evading the question. She clearly didn't want to talk any further about Tony.

Adesua could have pushed her friend to get the answers she was looking for. She'd like to hear what Fortune had to say, but she also felt a pull to remain loyal to Tony. She was planning to marry him … should she really be digging for information about him like this? Besides, Tony had said his previous relationships failed due to too many people getting involved.

She forced herself to let the conversation go. She would trust Tony and trust that God would guide their relationship, she decided.

With that decision, she smiled and intentionally shifted the conversation to something lighter, pushing her concerns aside.

On her way home, she was thinking about her discussion with Fortune and wondering what she knew about Tony. Fortune didn't seem happy about Tony, but Adesua didn't think she should press for information.

In the evening however, Fortune called Adesua and said, "I'd like to see you tomorrow, please." Her voice was quiet but firm.

Adesua hesitated, sensing something unusual. "Okay … but I'm just wondering, does this have something to do with Tony?" She asked, her curiosity now turning into mild concern.

"Don't ask me, Adesua." Fortune replied, her tone careful. "Where would you like us to meet?"

After a brief pause, Adesua agreed to come to Fortune's uncle's house again, at 7pm.

The next day, at 6:50pm, Adesua arrived at the house. After exchanging pleasantries with Fortune's uncle and his wife in the living room, Fortune led her into her bedroom so they could have a private conversation. She offered Adesua a can of juice and a straw, placing them on the table beside her.

"Thanks." Adesua said, opening the can and inserting the straw. She took a sip as they made small talk, but she couldn't help wondering what Fortune had called her over for.

Then, with a smile, she finally asked, "So, what's up? You said you'd like to see me."

Fortune didn't smile back. Instead, she took a deep breath and said, "Let's pray."

Adesua's smile disappeared, and her heart started to beat faster. Something about Fortune's tone disturbed her. Setting the can of juice down, she closed her eyes.

Fortune's prayer was short. She asked God to take control of their conversation, but it left Adesua feeling uneasy. *What was going on? What was she about to hear?*

After the prayer, Fortune's expression remained serious, almost concerned as she began to talk. "After our meeting yesterday, I called my pastor in Warri, and he gave me the go-ahead to talk to you."

Adesua sat up straight, her attention fully on Fortune.

Fortune continued, her words slow and deliberate. "I know Tony very well, and I think there are some things you need to know about him. Well, you may know them already, anyway."

Adesua leaned forward, her pulse quickening.

Fortune's gaze didn't waver. "I don't know what Tony has told you about himself, but… he's not real. He's a deceiver."

Adesua frowned, her mind racing. "What do you mean?"

Fortune shook her head. "Adesua, you can't marry him." She said, almost pleading.

The words hit Adesua like a punch in the stomach.

Fortune asked, "How did you meet him?"

"In church … my church!"

"Why am I not surprised?" Fortune commented. "He operates amongst the brethren."

"He operates amongst the brethren?! What do you mean? And why did you say I can't marry him?" Adesua asked, her voice shaky.

Fortune looked at her with deep concern. "When he was in Warri, he impregnated two women and then ran away."

Adesua's eyes widened. "In your church?!"

Fortune shook her head. "No, not in mine. He joined our church for a short while and left. Apparently, he couldn't stay—it was too hot for him. My pastor saw through him right away. He left and joined another church. One of the women he impregnated was a member of that church. The second one wasn't even a Christian."

Adesua was shocked. "Wha-t? Are you sure about what you're saying?"

Fortune nodded solemnly. "Yes, it's true. I'm not making this up."

"But … how could he have done that? I mean, he's a Christian." Adesua stammered, her mind scrambling for explanations.

Fortune sighed, shaking her head. "Tony's not a Christian. The Bible says by their fruits, we shall know them. Look at his actions."

Adesua's mind was racing as she tried to process the shocking information. "I can't believe this." She murmured, but even as the words left her lips, she knew in her heart that the news was most likely true.

And then, the truth began to unravel slowly, bit by bit.

"He also duped some people out of money." Fortune added.

The words hit Adesua and she almost fainted as her thoughts swirled with confusion.

Fortune continued, her voice steady. "After that, he suddenly disappeared. Apparently, he relocated and found a new place; a new church to operate in."

"But … why church?" Adesua asked, almost to herself.

Fortune shrugged. "It's baffling to me too. I guess churches are easy targets for people like him."

Still staring at her friend, Adesua spoke again, her voice barely above a whisper. "Are you sure we're talking about the same person?"

Fortune nodded; her expression unwavering. "I'm talking about Tony—the man in the picture you showed me yesterday. He knows me very well. You can mention my name to him."

Adesua opened her mouth to speak but closed it when no word came out. Her thoughts were spiraling. This was too much to take in all at once.

"He's a scammer, Adesua." Fortune added quietly. "I know some of the people he scammed. He lies about these businesses he's supposedly involved in, collects money from people, and never pays them back."

Adesua still didn't respond, her mind clouded with shock and disbelief. Had she lost her money?!

Fortune spoke again. "Hold on. I'll call someone now, maybe the person can explain better."

"No." Adesua said, shaking her head and raising a hand to stop her. She felt embarrassed already and didn't want to involve more people in this.

"I won't mention your name." Fortune assured her. "Just listen to the conversation."

Reluctantly, Adesua nodded, and Fortune dialed a number. After a few rings, someone picked up.

"A quick one … it's about Tony." Fortune began, her voice calm. "A friend of mine met him and now wants to marry him."

The female voice on the other end cut in sharply, "Marry Tony?! Tell your friend to flee. I hope she's not pregnant already. And I hope she hasn't given him any money."

As Adesua listened, she felt stupid.

"I don't know," Fortune replied and glanced at Adesua. "I haven't asked my friend about that."

"Well, talk to her. Tony is bad news." The female voice warned.

"Alright, thanks. I'll talk to you later. Bye." Fortune said and ended the call.

Adesua remained speechless, frozen in place.

"I'm sorry but I felt you should know." Fortune said sympathetically.

Adesua nodded, her mind still spinning from everything she had just heard.

"So, what are you going to do?" Fortune asked gently.

Adesua sighed, "I'll have to ask him."

Fortune nodded. "Okay. Keep me informed. I hope you haven't given him money."

Adesua hesitated for a moment before answering, "He asked me for loans for his business, and I gave him."

Fortune's eyes widened in disbelief. "What's wrong with him?!"

"Oh, you can be sure that I'll get my money back if all that you told me is true." Adesua stated confidently as she got up.

"You haven't finished your drink." Fortune pointed out.

Adesua glanced at the half-full can of juice and shook her head. "I can't drink any more."

Fortune stood and saw her off to her car. "Please, drive safely." She said.

As Adesua drove away, her thoughts were consumed by Tony, the man she thought she knew.

Should she go to his house now? She glanced at the clock on the dashboard. It was 9pm. She wanted nothing more than to confront him right now and get answers to the many questions on her mind, but she felt in her heart that she shouldn't. It didn't feel right to go at this time of the day, more so as her emotions were still raw. She was feeling very angry.

She decided to wait until tomorrow, even though she had no idea how she would be able to sleep at night with the burden on her mind. The pain in her heart seemed physical, as if she had been stabbed with a knife in her chest.

It would have been easier if she could talk to her family or friends, but since she didn't tell them that she was in a relationship with Tony, how could she involve them now? Later perhaps, if what she heard about Tony was true. She wasn't even sure what to believe yet.

As she drove on, her mind turned with fear, uncertainty, anger, and the uncomfortable realization that the man she thought she was going to marry might have been a stranger all along.

The next day, she went to the TV station. Concentrating and looking calm were difficult, but she managed. She was finally free to leave at 5pm, and she called Tony. She would need to know where he was.

After exchanging pleasantries, she casually asked if he was at home, and he said yes. *Good.* She wished him a wonderful evening and ended the call.

She decided to send a message to Nancy and Moyo in case something happened to her. With what she had just heard about Tony, she was no longer sure she was safe with him.

Just a heads-up: I'm going to Tony's house now.

Getting inside her car, she headed in the direction of his house.

When she arrived, Tony opened the door, looking surprised. "This is a surprise. You didn't tell me you'd be coming. What's going on?" His spoke casually, but there was a hint of unease in his voice.

"I'll explain. Can I come inside?" She said, her tone was soft but firm.

"Er ... yes, but … er … my sister is around." He replied, forcing a smile as if trying to ease the tension.

"Your sister?" Adesua raised an eyebrow. "Good, no problem. I'd like to meet her." She might be able to get some answers and help from his sister.

Tony's eyes darted nervously, and then glancing over his shoulder into the apartment, he called out, "Er, Adesua is here. She wants to meet you."

As Adesua stood in the doorway, waiting for him to move aside so she could enter the living room, she caught a glimpse of a woman in a spaghetti top and shorts retreating into his bedroom. Her heart skipped a beat. The lady looked familiar. Something wasn't right.

"Who is that lady?!" She demanded, her voice rising.

Tony blinked, feigning confusion. "Which lady?" A corner of his mouth turned up in a smile.

"The lady that went inside your bedroom just now!" Adesua said, her tone sharp with suspicion.

"I already told you, that's my sister."

Adesua's eyes narrowed as she scrutinized his face. "Your sister?" She echoed; her voice laced with doubt.

"Yes." He insisted and then stepped aside to let her in, his smile growing increasingly strained.

She entered the living room, but instead of sitting down, she stood firm, her eyes sweeping over the room. Her gaze landed on a pair of female bathroom slippers in a corner. She looked at Tony, her expression hardening. "The lady I just saw is not your sister. She looks like the lady I saw with you at my colleague's birthday ceremony."

Tony laughed, but it felt hollow. "No, she's not. Besides, you've never met my sister. How could you say she's not my sister?"

Adesua crossed her arms, her voice calm but unyielding. "Tony, I'm not a fool. Don't insult my intelligence."

Tony's laughter faded, but he said nothing, leaving the tension hanging in the air between them.

Adesua stared at him, heartbroken. She had been hoping that the things Fortune told her were not entirely true, but now, she believed everything. Tony had been deceiving her.

She would have loved to cause a scene by marching inside his bedroom to see the woman, but she knew she shouldn't. That wouldn't be right. If something should happen to her, she'd have herself to blame. Besides, Tony was not worth the trouble. The lady could have him.

"Okay, I'm here to discuss something with you. Would you please come?" She said firmly.

Without waiting for his response, she turned and headed toward the door.

Tony didn't argue but followed her, and quietly closed the door behind them.

In the hallway, he asked, "You look upset. What happened?"

She spun around to face him, her eyes cold. "Why didn't you tell me about the things that happened—the things you did in Warri?"

Tony's face tightened in what seemed like genuine confusion. "The things I did? What are you talking about?"

"You know what I mean!" She said in a sharp tone. "I heard you impregnated two women in Warri." Her eyes scanned his face for the truth.

Tony's eyes widened in what appeared to be a shock. "Who's feeding you these lies?" He demanded.

"Lies? Really?" Adesua shot back, her voice rising in frustration. "Who is Margaret? Who is Tina?"

Tony shook his head. "No, no. That's not what happened. I can explain, Adesua."

"Oh, so you know them. Good." She said and went on. "I also know you've been deceiving people to take money from them."

"That's not true!" Tony protested, his voice sounding defensive now.

He wanted to take Adesua's hand, but she took a step back.

"Tony, I don't trust you anymore. We're done. It's over." She said firmly. This was the end.

His face fell, and desperation crept into his voice. "Adesua, no, don't say that. I can explain. There's more to the story."

"I'd like to hear your side of the story, but not now. Right now, I want my money back!"

Tony hesitated, his eyes darting away for a moment before he looked back at her. "I already used it for the business. I can take you to the site of the project and show you where your money went."

"I don't care about the site! I care about my money! If you really have nothing to hide, you'll find a way to repay me!"

Tony opened his mouth to respond but then shut it, uncertainty showing in his eyes.

"I'll be expecting my money!"

With that, Adesua turned. As she walked toward the stairs, she heard him calling her name, but she didn't turn back, and he didn't try to pursue her.

Inside her car, she burst into tears, her heart shattered. How could this have happened to her? *Lord, why did you allow this to happen to me*? Her heart cried.

When she was calm, she started her car and drove away.

But where could she go? She couldn't face her family in this state. The moment she stepped through the door, they would know something was wrong and start asking her questions. She wasn't ready for those questions. And what could she possibly say to them now? She knew she would need to reveal everything to her family, but not now. This evening wasn't the time.

What she needed now was a place where she would be able to weep freely.

Nancy. Yes, Nancy.

With trembling hands, Adesua pulled out her phone and dialed her friend's number.

The phone rang just once before Nancy picked up. "Hello?"

"Nancy ... are you home?" Adesua's voice cracked.

Nancy barely recognized her voice. "I am. What's going on? You sound—"

"I'm coming now. Please call Moyo. Ask her where she is."

"Okay, I'll call her. But Adesua, what's—"

"I'll explain when I get there," Adesua cut in quickly.

"Okay."

CHAPTER 8

IT WASN'T LONG before Adesua arrived at Nancy's house. Nancy opened the door and a look at Adesua's face told her she had been crying. Without asking any question, she ushered Adesua inside and led her straight to her room.

Moyo was still on the way, but Nancy called her and put the phone on speaker.

As Adesua told them what had happened, they expressed shock.

"Adesua, why didn't you tell us?" Moyo asked.

"Do you ... do you think he hypnotized you?" Nancy wanted to know because she found it difficult to believe that Adesua allowed such things to happen.

Adesua shook her head. "I don't think so ... I mean … I don't know how I could have believed him for so long." She said through her tears.

"Have you told your parents?" Moyo asked.

Another shake of the head.

"They need to know." Nancy insisted as she rubbed Adesua's back gently.

"Yes, I know." Adesua's voice was almost a whisper now as the reality of what she would have to do pressed in on her.

Moyo asked Adesua to wait for her at Nancy's house.

When she arrived, they discussed and agreed that she should inform her parents immediately, and also report to the pastor before taking any other action. Moyo was ready to get Tony arrested.

It was nearly 10pm when Adesua finally left Nancy's house. The drive home was a blur of emotions for her. She couldn't believe that the man she loved and thought was a Christian had deceived her so thoroughly. He had conned her all along, and she had bought it hook, line and sinker. She believed him. It never occurred to her that such a man could be inside church. She had opened up her heart and hand to him, but he had repaid her with pain. This pain was a wound that would take a long time to heal, she was sure.

Around 9.30am the next day, she received a message from Tony.

I didn't mean to hurt you.

She replied.

Okay, but I want my money back.

He called her. "I told you it's been spent!"

"I don't care! Give me my money back!" She shouted.

"I don't have it."

"Tony?!"

"Please calm down. Let's try to resolve this misunderstanding. We're in a relationship."

"There's no relationship. It's over."

"No, stop saying that." He said.

He asked her who had told her those things about him, but she refused to reveal the source. She didn't think that mattered.

Then, he said, "I still want to marry you, and my feelings haven't changed." He paused for a moment before adding, "Can I come to your office so we can talk?"

"No, I'm not interested in any discussion. Just return my money." She insisted.

"Well, I don't have it right now, but I'll try to get it back to you." He responded weakly.

"You have to. I'm not going to let you get away with it!"

She ended the call. What happened afterward was a combination of tears, despair, anger, and embarrassment. Tony was a liar, a deceiver. The relationship she believed she had was a total lie. The man she thought he was didn't exist.

She was back to point zero, and the thought of this made her burst into tears.

She had come close to getting married again. And again, the relationship had failed … Well, that was if she could count Tony and the relationship as real. The first time she got close to getting married was at the age of twenty three. She wasn't ready to be married, and she ended the relationship. Now that she was ready, things were not working well for her.

She still found it difficult to believe that she had been swindled by Tony. She regretted not listening to the voice of God that warned her.

In the afternoon, Adesua sent Tony a message. It was short and to the point.

I need my money back!

Her heart raced as she pressed send, knowing that this would be the final communication between them.

He called almost immediately, but she didn't pick up. There was nothing left to say. Whatever explanations or excuses he had, she didn't want to hear them.

In the evening, she gathered her family—her parents and sisters—around the living room, and recounted everything … the relationship, the lies, the money, and Tony's life in Warri.

Efua was the first to speak while her parents exchanged shocked glances. "You were in a relationship with him? And you gave him that amount of money?!" Her voice was filled with disbelief.

Noredia seemed too stunned to speak.

"I almost can't believe you hid this from us … from me." Her mother eventually said.

Her mother wanted to know some things and she answered.

"When are you seeing your pastor?" Her father finally asked.

"Tomorrow," Adesua replied quietly.

"Let us know what the church decides." His voice was calm, but it was obvious that he was very upset.

"Okay, Dad."

He spoke again, his eyes narrowing slightly. "Do you have any message or document that shows the money was a loan?"

Adesua shook her head. She had nothing to say; she knew she made a terrible mistake.

Her father's frown deepened, disbelief clouding his expression. "You gave him over two million naira without any written agreement? No proof? Not even a text message?!"

"I transferred the money to him. Is my bank statement proof enough?"

"Bank statement is not a proof that it's a loan." He said. "Well, we'll see how it goes, although it may not end the way you hope."

She sighed. Yesterday, she had told Tony she wasn't a fool, but as she listened to her father now, she realized she had been one, after all.

The next day, she went to her church to report to Pastor Andrew.

The part about the money made the man angry. He said when the church needed funds recently, Adesua contributed very little.

"That was what I could afford at the time, sir." She replied.

"But you gave over two million to Tony." He shot back, glaring at her.

"The money was meant for something specific." She explained. "I gave it to him because he said he urgently needed it for his business."

"Well, I don't want to say you got what you deserved, but you should have given more to the church." He told her.

Adesua took a deep breath, staying silent.

He then said he would talk to Tony to get his side of the story. He asked her to come back to see him on Monday.

Adesua thanked him, but as she left his office, she doubted she would get a positive response from him. She didn't think he would be able to help her.

She was back in his office on Monday and he said that Tony told him the monies were gifts from her.

"Gifts?!" She had not expected to hear that.

He nodded. "He did not deny that he collected money from you twice, but he said they were gifts from you, and he used the monies for his business."

"That's not true. How can over two million be a gift?" She pointed out. Her heart ached as the realization of everything began to sink in. The man she had thought she would marry was not who he seemed.

"Well, that's what he said. Now, it's your word against his."

"Since he didn't deny collecting money from me, he should return it." She decided.

Pastor Andrew advised her to be patient with Tony to pay it back. "He won't leave the church."

He also said that Tony admitted he was economical with the truth concerning the things that happened in Warri.

Adesua frowned. "Economical with the truth? He didn't tell me any truth. He did not say a word about the things that happened in Warri."

Pastor Andrew continued, explaining that Tony had admitted some things happened in Warri, though not exactly what Adesua had been told. Tony also expressed that he still wanted to marry her, but blamed her for believing the person who shared those things about him.

Tony is evil, Adesua thought as she sat in astonished silence. She could hardly believe she had once believed he was a Christian and had agreed to marry him. The marriage would have been a disaster.

At home, she told her father all that Pastor Andrew told her. Her father said they could get Tony arrested and charged to court, but he didn't think it was worth it.

He went on. "We can pursue the case though if you want, but I don't think I want you to."

He blamed Adesua for all that had happened, and also said that Pastor Andrew did not handle things right. "I think you should leave that church."

Devastated, Adesua decided to take three days off work. Tony had used her, and she felt like a fool. He did not apologize or admit anything but was just giving excuses. The only thing he admitted was that he was economical with the truth.

For days, she cried whenever she was alone. She felt dazed. She also felt hopeless about the future. She was beautiful, but here she was, still single. Was she destined to be alone?

At the end of the three days, she returned to work. Her body had rested, but not her mind or emotions. She felt undesirable, foolish, vulnerable, used and dumped.

On set though, she covered it well; she was her usual, laughing, cool, calm, and professional self. But inside, she felt broken, totally discouraged.

In the days that followed, she leaned on her friends and family for support. As she began to feel better, she began the process of moving on, determined to rebuild her life, rebuild her bank account, and protect her heart from further pain.

But going to church became a struggle for her because Tony was still there, and every time she saw him, a fresh wave of pain came over her. Pastor Andrew's seeming indifference in his handling of the situation didn't help her either, and she was now questioning some things about the church. She began to feel disconnected.

CHAPTER 9

BY THE FOLLOWING month, confusion and bitterness seemed to have taken root in Adesua's heart. She didn't know what she believed anymore, or how to make sense of everything happening around her.

Realizing she needed help, she decided to go with her family to their church on Sunday; perhaps a change of environment would help her. When she told her family she would worship in their church on Sunday, July 2nd, they were happy.

On the way to church that Sunday morning, her mind went to Jimi. She hadn't thought about him in a long time, but today, his face floated to the surface of her mind. When they broke up and he left the church, she couldn't understand why, but now she understood.

In the sermon preached by the senior pastor of the church, Adesua was reminded that people might not know what she was going through, but that was not true of Jesus. He knew and wanted to help her; to help the broken hearted.

The first scripture that was read was *Matthew 12:20 NKJV.*

A bruised reed He will not break, And smoking flax He will not quench, Till He sends forth justice to victory;

Another scripture was read.

Hosea 13:9 KJV
O Israel, thou hast destroyed thyself; but in Me is thine help.

She had chosen to sit toward the back of the church, away from her family members because she didn't want to be seen by the senior pastor of the church and his wife as they knew her very well.

And so, she was surprised when the service ended and an usher told her that the senior pastor would like to see her. Apparently, he had sighted her.

Carrying her handbag, she went to the pastor's office. His wife, Pastor Mosun, was there, and they greeted her warmly, happy to see her in their church again. They wanted to know how she had been doing, and she said she'd been doing well. She remarked that the sermon blessed her.

The senior pastor prayed briefly for her, and she left.

At home later, she reflected on the day's sermon. She had been blaming Tony, blaming herself, and even Pastor Andrew, but she realized she needed to let go of the hurt, pain, and her mistakes … and focus on her walk with God. What she needed was a closer relationship with God.

By Wednesday, she had decided to return to the church where her parents and siblings worshipped, Solid Rock Bible Church. One of her reasons for leaving the church was that it did not have air conditioning, but that changed with its installation last year.

When she told Moyo and Nancy of her decision, they tried to convince her to stay, but her mind was made up.

The following Sunday, she was back in the church with her family, and this time, she sat with them. While she listened to the powerful sermon being preached by the senior pastor, she decided to create time to be in God's presence. She needed to think, learn from the past, hear God, and understand where He was taking her. She planned not to attend any social event for a week unless it was absolutely necessary.

That week, she read the Bible, worshipped the Lord, and prayed in her understanding and tongues. She also listened to the senior pastor's sermons online.

As she did these things, some things came to her spirit, and she wrote them in the note on her iPad. The last things she wrote in the note were:

Those failed relationships were not part of God's plans for me.

The relationships failed, but God didn't fail, and He was firmly in control still.

Desperation pushed me into a relationship with Tony. All the warning signs of a wrong relationship were there, but I chose to ignore them. I must not allow that to happen again.

When I realized Tony had deceived me, I asked God, "Why did You allow this to happen to me?" Now, I see that

God had tried to warn me multiple times, but I refused to listen.

Without realizing it, I had become proud, convinced that I knew everything and no longer needed guidance.

As she wrote the final words, she whispered a prayer, asking the Holy Spirit to teach her humility.

The following Sunday, she was in church, and when she returned home, she ate and went to her room. She prayed and feeling tired, she slept.

Suddenly, she woke up from a dream. She couldn't remember the details, but she heard a voice say to her - *when are you going to ask Me what I want you to do with your life?*

Where did that come from?! Could that be God? *God*?!

As she considered the words, she knew it must be God, and tears slipped from her eyes. Slowly, she got up from the bed and went on her knees. With her head resting on the bed, she asked God to forgive and help her. A song came to her mind, and she began to sing it.

I'm coming back to the heart of worship
And it's all about You
It's all about You, Jesus
I'm sorry, Lord, for the things I've made it
When it's all about You
It's all about You, Jesus.

After some time, she got up to lay back in bed, but she couldn't sleep again. Deciding to read the Bible, she took her iPad, and opened the Bible App. The pastor preached from the Acts of the Apostles chapter eight in church in the morning, and she decided to read the whole of the chapter. Within minutes, she was through, and she went to chapter nine. As she read verse six, she felt the Holy Spirit whispering in her ears, and she stopped to consider the words of the verse carefully.

Acts 9:6 NKJV
[6] So he, trembling and astonished, said, "Lord, what do You want me to do?" Then the Lord said to him, "Arise and go into the city, and you will be told what you must do."

She wasn't sure what she was supposed to learn from the verse, but she felt compelled to say the same words to God, and she began, "Lord, what do You want me to do? Reveal Your will to me in Jesus' name."

Afterward, she kept silent and listened to hear what God would say to her, but she didn't hear anything. The only thing that occurred to her was to see the pastor's wife, Pastor Mosun, to discuss with her. The woman would listen and counsel her appropriately, she was sure.

She would also need to join a department in the church and begin to serve. She wouldn't like to be a bench warmer, but which department would she join? Before she left the church to join *God's Word Assembly*, she went through the

Worker's Class and belonged to the Technical Department. She wondered if she should return to that Department.

When she discussed with her sisters the next day, they told her to see Pastor Mosun. She was in charge of all the departments, and Adesua wouldn't be able to join a department without the woman's approval. Adesua told them she had planned to see Pastor Mosun on Sunday.

After service on Sunday, she went in the direction of Pastor Mosun's office. The pastor was attending to someone and while Adesua waited at the reception, she used her phone.

She watched a video on YouTube and afterward started reading the viewers' comments.

Someone wrote:

A lady met a tall, handsome, educated consultant who wore a three-piece suit, glasses, and carried a briefcase, while shopping at a mall. While talking to her, he mentioned that he was still very upset with his family for committing him to a psychiatric institution a year ago. The lady quickly ran away. Listen, there are real-life successful and handsome lunatics out there!

Adesua smiled. *That's very true*, she had encountered one of them—Tony.

Before long, she was called, and she entered the pastor's office.

Deciding to open up, she told Pastor Mosun about some of the mistakes she had made in her relationship with Jimi, and then with Tony.

She also related to the woman the dream she had some days ago. "I know that was God speaking to me."

Pastor Mosun agreed, and after counseling her, she prayed for her.

Afterward, Adesua revealed that she had decided to return to the church and would like to join a department.

Pastor Mosun was happy to hear that, but she said Adesua would need to go through the Worker's Class again, which would take two months.

Adesua pointed out that she went through the class before she left the church. Did she have to go through it again?

Pastor Mosun said yes. That was the rule in the church. Besides, some other things had been added to the manual.

Adesua wanted to protest, but she heard the Holy Spirit tell her to shut up, and she did. *Didn't you ask Me to teach you humility* - she heard Him say. *Ah! Yes, I did.*

She nodded and told Pastor Mosun that she understood. She agreed to go through the class and promised to start the following Sunday.

As Pastor Mosun continued speaking, Adesua felt a stirring in her heart, a desire to submit and serve this woman in any way possible. It would be a privilege.

The next Sunday, Adesua started the class, and week after week, every Sunday afternoon, she was in the class, her attention unwavering. With each session, she began to see why Pastor Mosun had insisted she go through the class again. It wasn't just about the teachings, it was about renewing her mindset, grounding herself in humility, and preparing her heart for more of God.

Pastor Mosun kept in touch with her, to encourage her and know how she was doing. During one of such meetings, Adesua expressed her desire to serve in her office. Pastor Mosun was pleased to hear that, and she shared the expectations with her.

Adesua eventually completed the class and began to serve as one of Pastor Mosun's Personal Assistants in October.

She continued praying with Moyo and Nancy every Monday, and when they got married in November and December respectively, she served as their maid of honor.

****

Tade was driving his father's Toyota car that Sunday morning, the second Sunday of March; he was on his way to *Solid Rock Bible Church*. He had been invited to the church by the pastor, to minister in song. The pastor's wife, Pastor Mosun, was his aunt. Tade had promised to arrive by 9am, the time the service would start, even though he wouldn't be called up to sing until around 11am. As he navigated the slow traffic caused by an accident, he glanced at the dashboard clock; the time was now 8.40am. With the traffic moving at a snail's pace, he doubted he'd make it to the church on time.

He grabbed his phone and called Pastor Mosun to inform her of the delay. After asking for the color of his car, she informed him that he would find two of the church's protocol officers by the church's gate. After the call, he began to speak in tongues as the traffic slowly edged forward.

He eventually arrived at the church at 9.25am. Two protocol officers were waiting for him by the gate, and he was directed to a reserved parking spot. As he parked the car, he could hear someone praying inside the church hall. Exiting the car, he greeted the men warmly, and followed them, with his Bible and phone in his hands.

Just as they stepped inside the hall, a woman announced that it was time to praise and worship the Lord. Tade was taken to the front where Pastor Mosun and her husband were, and he greeted them. He was shown his seat which was right beside his aunt's. He put his Bible on the small table in front of him and remained standing, to join the congregation to sing.

Thirty-year-old Tade was slightly light skinned and tall, with short hair. He went to a university in Ghana where he studied law. He had wanted to be a medical doctor, but when he suddenly discovered that he couldn't stand the sight of blood, he changed his mind and went for law. After passing his Bar exam, he chose to stay back in Ghana, and got a job at Nkrumah, Davids & Simone Law Firm. Despite how he became a lawyer, he liked practicing law. He also liked living in Ghana. He was doing well, had his own accommodation, and came to Nigeria twice or thrice every year. His mother was late, but his father and only sibling sometimes visited him in Ghana.

When Tade left Nigeria and went to Ghana at the age of seventeen, he wasn't a Christian. Three years after, Pastor Mosun who was his late mother's younger sister was invited to preach in a church in Ghana. When she arrived, he went to see her at the guest house she was lodged in, and she invited him to attend the event. He didn't want to attend, but she was able to persuade him. Reluctantly, he went, with the plan to leave as soon as Pastor Mosun finished speaking. As it happened, a man preached before Pastor Mosun and when the man gave an altar call, Tade went forward to give his life to Christ. When the event finally ended, he went to his aunt who took him to the pastor of the church and introduced Tade as her nephew and one of the new believers. Tade joined the church, became baptized in the Holy Spirit and water, and began to serve in the church. Pastor Mosun kept in touch with him, and whenever he came to Nigeria on vacation, she made sure she saw him.

Tade was now one of the Assistant Pastors in the church, and the minister in charge of the music department. He was a very good singer, and sometimes sang with the choir. The church had its headquarters in Nigeria. His father and younger brother had also become Christians and attended a church.

When Tade spoke with his aunt last month, he disclosed that he would be coming to Nigeria for his church's annual convention which was compulsory for all pastors and ministers to attend. The convention would take a week, and he would spend another two weeks, before returning to Ghana.

Pastor Mosun discussed with her husband, and they asked Tade if he could come to their church to sing on the Sunday after the convention, and he happily accepted the invitation.

Pastor Mosun also asked if he had found a woman he'd like to marry. He laughed and when he said there was no one yet, she encouraged him to seek God's face about it.

Tade arrived for the convention and stayed in his father's house. The event went well and ended last Sunday.

And now, he was in his aunt's church which was his second time in the church. He was there four years ago, but did not sing then.

At 11.10, it was time for him to sing, and the person who had been playing the keyboard got up. Tade was introduced, and he left his seat. Collecting the microphone, he appreciated the Senior Pastors of the church for the opportunity. He also talked briefly about how he became a Christian and the difference that Christ makes in a life.

Then he walked to the keyboard, sat down, and led the congregation to worship the Lord with songs. At the end, he gave altar call, and three people came forward. They were prayed for, and as Tade returned to his seat, people clapped to appreciate him.

When the service attended, Tade saw a beautiful tall lady approach his aunt. With a smile, the lady bent down and carried Pastor Mosun's handbag and Bible.

The pastor glanced at the lady with appreciation and Tade heard her say, "Thank you, Adesua." And then turning to Tade, the pastor said, "Let's go to my office."

Adesua was in front, and Tade and his aunt followed her down the hallway. When Adesua reached the door of the office, she brought out a key with which she unlocked the door, and they all entered the office.

Adesua placed the handbag and Bible on the table, and stepped back so the woman could get to her seat. She waited for Tade to sit down, and then she asked him, "What would you like to drink, sir?"

She mentioned the choices available, and Tade said water was fine.

As Adesua moved around, bringing out the refreshments that had been bought, and setting them on the table, something about her conduct caught Tade's attention. She had a combination of grace and manners, and he looked at her curiously.

When she finished, she excused herself and exited the office, leaving the pastor and Tade alone.

Tade glanced at the table and saw plates of rice, chicken, fish, two bottles of water, a bottle of orange juice, napkins, glass cups, and cutleries.

Pastor Mosun blessed the food, and as she took a fork, she explained that her husband was fasting that day and would not be eating until later. If he wasn't fasting, they would have gone to his office or he would come over so they could eat together, she explained.

Tade nodded. He would keep that information in mind for his own marriage.

Smiling, he spoke again. "I'm surprised that someone as polished and beautiful as Adesua is serving as your Personal Assistant."

She nodded. "A Christian who is truly submitted to God should be willing and able to serve in any capacity, as a way to honor God."

"That's true." He agreed.

There was silence for some seconds and then he asked, "Is she married or single?"

"Single. I'm actually trusting God for a good man for her."

"Wow! She seems like a nice lady."

"She is." Pastor Mosun confirmed, and looking at him, she smiled knowingly and asked, "Would you like me to introduce you properly?"

He laughed and said *Okay* casually with a shrug, but he was excited. He'd like to get to know Adesua better.

When they finished eating, Pastor Mosun called her secretary. The lady came to clear the table and as she was leaving the room, she asked the lady to call Adesua for her.

Adesua soon returned to the office, and Pastor Mosun introduced her to Tade with a friendly tone. Looking at Adesua, she said, "As was announced during service, this is my nephew."

"Yes, Pastor. You also told me sometime ago that one of your nephews lived in Ghana." Adesua said.

"Yes, this is he. He's a lawyer. He studied in Ghana and decided to stay back." And then looking at Tade, she pointed at Adesua. "This is Adesua. She's the host of The Adesua Show on JKITV."

"Is that a TV show?"

"Yes."

"That's impressive." Tade stood and held out a hand with a smile. "I'm glad to meet you."

Adesua took the hand. "I'm glad to meet you, too." With her shoes, they were about the same height.

As Tade sat down, he wanted to know how long she'd been working in television, and she said she'd been in it for a few years now.

"Wow! Interesting. I've always been curious about how that works." He said.

Pastor Mosun said she'd like to see some of the members before they left the church, and she stood up. As she walked past Adesua, she said, "Please, sit down." Then she left the room.

Adesua sat on the couch that was there, and Tade turned his chair to face her.

He asked some questions, and she began to share some things about the media world and her show. He could see that she was very intelligent. She also loved what she did.

As they conversed easily, Adesua felt there was something impressive about this man who was soft spoken. There was a gentleness and kindness about him, yet a quiet strength.

Then he asked for her phone number. "I'd like to call you before I return to Ghana."

They exchanged phone numbers.

Few minutes after, as they were wrapping up their conversation, Pastor Mosun returned to the office. "Is everything going okay?"

Tade smiled and nodded. "Yes."

He told his aunt he would like to leave. She gave him an envelope as honorarium, and while she saw him off, Adesua removed his used glass cup and wiped the table.

♥ CHAPTER 10

THE DRIVE HOME took about fifty minutes. After lunch and some time with his father and brother, Tade went to his room. Making himself comfortable in bed, he took his phone and went on YouTube. He typed Adesua's name, and some videos came up. He chose one, touched play, and was immediately faced with Adesua as she started the show and welcomed her viewers.

As he watched with a thoughtful expression on his face, he couldn't help but admire her. She was captivating in a way that was hard to explain. Aside being beautiful, she was so poised, confident, and articulate. It was obvious she had a lot going for her and was doing well. It was also obvious that she was a committed Christian.

Going by what his aunt had said, she was not in a relationship, and he wondered why she was still single. She seemed like someone who would have plenty of options, and yet, here she was—still single. Well, he knew that Christians must be led by God, and they must listen for His guidance in every decision.

It occurred to him that people might be saying the same thing about him, wondering why he hadn't found a woman to marry yet, and he chuckled quietly.

He continued watching her and thought that there was something about her that intrigued him.

The show was very interesting and engaging, and when it ended, he closed YouTube and called his aunt.

"I've just finished watching one of her shows. It's very interesting; she's very good." He remarked. "I'm surprised she's not yet in a relationship. Is she picky?" Was she looking for a man who was a little more intellectual?

"No, not really. She's had some relationships that didn't work. Now, she just wants the will of God. Of course, such a man must be godly and be able to make sound decisions."

As they talked, he laughed.

Then he said he had collected her phone number. "I'll probably give her a call tomorrow."

She advised him to send a message to Adesua first as she didn't usually pick unknown numbers. She also advised him to pray before trying to get close to her as she wouldn't want him to raise Adesua's hopes unnecessarily.

"And keep me informed before taking any step because Adesua is my church member." She added.

"Well, when I call her, I'd like to invite her to lunch, depending on how the call goes." He quickly revealed.

After the call with his aunt, he closed his eyes, deep in thought. He replayed the conversation with his aunt in his mind. "She just wants the will of God ... a godly man, able to make sound decisions." Wasn't that what he wanted too? To find a woman who did not only share his values, but was also grounded in faith, intelligent, and could walk alongside him in life.

His aunt's advice lingered in his mind. "Pray before getting close to her." *Hmm.*

Adesua.

She was beautiful, charming, smart, and successful, but was she who he needed? Would they be compatible? Was this interest in Adesua something God was orchestrating, or was it just his own curiosity?

He brought out his phone. He had saved her number in his contacts, and he looked her up on WhatsApp. He found her and looked at her profile picture for about a minute. Then he began to type.

Hi,

He stopped when he felt in his spirit that he shouldn't rush to contact her.

Deciding to slow down and pray instead, he put his phone down. He breathed deeply and began to talk to God. "Lord, if this is from You, let me know. If it's not, give me the heart and wisdom to step back, in Jesus' name."

He didn't contact her that evening, but around noon the following day, he sent a message.

Hi, this is Tade. How's your day going?

If she replied, he'd know she wasn't very busy, and he would call her right away.

When there was no reply, he guessed she was not available.

****

Adesua eventually responded in the evening. She was inside her car, about to leave the TV station.

Hi. Good to hear from you. My day's been good, thank you. How about you? Hope you're enjoying yourself?

Tade, who had been monitoring his phone saw her message and responded immediately.

Yes, I am. Are you back at home?

No, not yet. I'm just leaving.

Can I call you now?

Yes.

Almost immediately, her phone began to buzz. She answered it, and they began to converse, starting with their day.

He said he'd been watching her shows on YouTube.

"Really? Thank you. That's good to know."

"You've gained at least a fan. I'll tune in on Friday to watch in real time."

She thanked him again. "That means a lot to me. For how long will you be around?"

"I'll be heading back on Saturday." He answered. "I'd like us to have lunch together before I do, if that's possible. Let me know the day and time you'll be available."

"Oh, okay. I'll check my schedule and get back to you."

"Sounds good."

They talked for some minutes more and then she said goodnight.

"Bye for now. Talk to you soon." He told her.

After the call, she looked thoughtful as she considered their conversation. *Lunch with him*?! That would be nice, but what she felt was a mixture of excitement and caution. She had to be careful as she wouldn't want her heart to be broken again.

Well, if she would go to lunch with him, she'd need to inform Pastor Mosun, after all, Tade was the pastor's nephew and she met him through her, just yesterday. But before that, she needed to answer a question … would she like to have lunch with him?

She let out a small sigh. "I'm not desperate. Lord, lead me, in Jesus' name."

She continued thinking and praying about Tade and his invitation until she got home.

Moments later at home, she called Pastor Mosun to inform her, and she said it was okay. She counseled Adesua to pray and if she was available, she could go.

Adesua stylishly asked the pastor some questions about Tade, and she was assured that he was a good and godly man, with good intentions.

She decided to accept the invitation. She would be careful and prayerful, not fearful. She had been keeping to herself since Tony's saga, but she would not allow fear in her heart. And for the first time in a while, she was open to the possibility of a meaningful relationship.

She told her mother and sisters about it, as she had resolved not to hide something as important as a potential relationship from the people who loved her … even if nothing came out of this meeting with Tade. They were all surprised but excited that it was Tade, Pastor Mosun's nephew.

****

The next morning, Tade called his aunt to let her know what he had discussed with Adesua, and she said she had been informed by Adesua. "She called me to let me know."

"That's good." He said. "I was wondering if you could help me with something. Do you have any restaurant suggestions? Somewhere she'd like?"

Pastor Mosun chuckled. "Funny you should ask. Adesua and I have talked about restaurants before. As a matter of fact, she's the one who books restaurants for the church's special guests, so I have a good idea of the kind of places she likes."

"Good." Tade said, relieved. He wanted the lunch to go smoothly, especially since this could be the first step toward something more. "Could you send me a few recommendations, please?"

"Sure. I'll forward some names to you on WhatsApp. That way, you can pick whichever works best for you both."

"Thanks, Auntie. I'll keep you updated."

He was still expecting the names when he got a message from Adesua, to give him day and time for the lunch.

He called her immediately. "Which restaurant would you prefer?"

"Anyone you choose is fine … as long as it's safe, decent, and the food is not bad." She said and chuckled. She no longer cared about being taken to one of the best rated restaurants in town as she once did.

"Got you." He chuckled, and then mentioned the name of a restaurant a friend talked about sometime ago.

Adesua knew the restaurant and knew it was expensive. She said, "Er … it doesn't have to be an expensive one. I frequent such places due to my job. Also, I'd prefer a dinner if it's okay with you. Afternoon time might not work well for me."

"Got you." He agreed.

Just then, he received his aunt's message, and he quickly opened it. Looking at it, he mentioned the name of the first restaurant, and Adesua said it was fine.

They discussed how to meet and when he said his father's car was available for him to use, she said he could pick her up at home. He agreed and she texted her address to him.

Good, everything seemed to be going on well, he thought. Still, he reminded himself to approach this thoughtfully, knowing that both of them were looking for something deeper than just casual outing. He would need to pray more.

That Wednesday, he came to her house to pick her up. Her parents were in the living room, and they greeted him warmly. He wore a light blue button-down shirt on jeans.

"Adesua mentioned you're a lawyer in Ghana. What's the name of your law firm?" Adesua's father asked him.

Tade answered politely, giving the name of his firm.

"And what's your area of specialization?" Her father continued.

Tade explained his focus in law, detailing the areas he practiced.

Adesua's mother said, "Thank you for leading that worship session on Sunday. It was truly uplifting. A lawyer and a worshipper … what a wonderful combination!"

Smiling, Tade thanked her.

Adesua was beautiful in the pink and white dress she wore. Her hair was held back with a pink hair band, her shoes and handbag were pink, and small pink earrings studded her ears.

They said goodbye to her parents and as they walked toward the door, he could smell her perfume. Outside, the gateman opened the gate and soon, they were on their way.

He wanted to know if her father was a lawyer.

Adesua nodded. "Yes, he is," she said, then mentioned the name of his law firm.

Tade's face lit up in recognition. "So, that's him! Wow, I know the firm!"

As he drove on, their conversation shifted to their families. She learned that his father was a businessman and his brother worked in a bank. They continued talking and laughing, exchanging stories.

At the restaurant, he parked the car close to the entrance, and they got down. The door was opened from inside, and as they threaded their way through the tables toward a table for two by a window, a man who sat at a table by himself stood to greet her. "Good to see you, Adesua. I watch your show."

Adesua responded nicely with a smile.

Tade noticed that some people were watching them as they passed through.

At their table, they sat down, and a waiter came to take their drink orders. As he was leaving, Adesua's phone began to ring. She glanced at it, cut it, and looked up.

"Do people always recognize you?" Tade asked her with a smile and a look of admiration.

"No, not always. It depends on where I am." She answered.

Before long, their food was served and they ate and conversed.

She wanted to know how he was doing in Ghana, and where he worked and worshipped.

As he responded, smiling, she could see that he was a solid Christian as his aunt had told her. He was also intelligent, with a good sense of humor. She tried to determine his age, and guessed he would be around her age, or a couple of years older.

When she asked if he planned to relocate to Nigeria anytime soon, he laughed and said he wasn't sure yet, but that God would lead him.

The conversation continued flowing easily.

When they eventually finished eating and the bill was brought, she asked to see it. She wanted to pay for herself, but he wouldn't let her.

He laughed. "I invited you. Why should you pay?"

He paid and they left. About fifty minutes after, they reached her house, and she got down. She thanked him and he left.

****

In bed later, Adesua was thinking about Tade. She liked everything about him and liked how his smile lit up his eyes.

She continued thinking of him and smiling until she fell asleep.

****

Tade called Adesua again two days after, and they spoke for about thirty minutes.

The morning of his departure, as Tade was finishing his final packing, his phone rang. It was Adesua. He smiled and answered quickly. "Good morning, Adesua."

"Good morning, Tade. This is just to wish you a safe flight back to Ghana." She said and then prayed briefly for him.

"Thank you. I appreciate that." He replied. "I'll keep in touch once I land."

"Alright. Take care."

Later in the afternoon, after his plane touched down in Accra, as he made his way through the usual post-flight routine, he sent her a quick message.

I'm back in Accra, and on my way home now.

She replied.
Praise God. Rest well and keep safe.

He got a cab, and soon was on his way home, with his thoughts still lingering on Adesua. At home, he ate, showered, and got in bed. It was good to be back.

He called some of his friends and a colleague at work, to let them know he had returned. They wanted to know if he had a good time in Nigeria, and he said a definite yes.

Afterward, he sent a message to Adesua and when she said she was back at home, he decided to call her. "Can I do a WhatsApp video call?"

"Video?"

When he said yes, she asked him to give her about three minutes. She was in the living room, and she went inside her bedroom. She looked at herself in the mirror and when she was ready, she called him on WhatsApp video.

"Hi," she said, her eyes brightening.

"Hi. How was your day?"

"It was busy, but good. How was your flight?"

They talked and laughed, and then prayed briefly.

On Monday, he wore black suit and tie, and went to work. The office occupied the first floor of a two-story building, with *Nkrumah, Davids & Simone Law Firm* boldly written on the front door in gold letters.

After greeting everyone, he entered his office. A side of the wall had two tall bookcases filled with volumes of law books. He sat at his table and prayed briefly, ready to dive back into his work.

CHAPTER 11

IN THE EVENING, Adesua was in the living room, eating dinner when she received Tade's call, and they talked for some minutes.

On Saturday afternoon, she sent a message to say hello and he replied.

He sent another message to know where she was, and when she said she was at home, he called her on WhatsApp video.

"What are you doing?" He asked, looking at her familiar face on the phone.

"Nothing. I'm just lying in bed in my room."

That surprised him, and she said, "I enjoy moments of isolation; when I'm just relaxing. I need it to clear my head."

"What do you do to relax?"

She giggled. "If I'm not lying in bed, speaking in tongues or reading the Bible, I love to read Christian romance novels or watch Christian movies." She paused, and then added, "I sometimes play games on my phone, although it's not often."

"Noted."

They continued talking and then he asked, "So, is there a man who wouldn't be pleased that I'm talking to you?"

Adesua's voice came through with a laugh. "Just ask if I'm in a relationship."

They both laughed.

"So?" He pressed, smiling.

She paused for a brief moment before answering, "No, I'm not in a relationship. What about you?" She asked in return.

"No." He admitted.

"Have you not met the right woman?" She teased, her curiosity now matching his.

He laughed again. "Well, you could say that. And the years just seem to fly by."

He thought for a moment, then added, "There are some wonderful ladies in my church, but somehow, I've never felt drawn to any of them. Recently, I've been praying and thinking more seriously about marriage, you know, really seeking God's will. What about you?"

"It's similar for me. I've been in relationships, but none that I believe God wanted for me. Now, I'm waiting and trusting His timing."

"Why didn't the relationships work?" He felt his way along, wondering if indeed she was the right woman for him.

She decided to tell him a little about Jimi and Tony. As she did, she also wondered if God had brought him into her life for a reason.

Their conversation quickly moved to birthdays and age. When she mentioned that she turned twenty nine on November 12th, Tade smiled and replied, "I'm about nine months older than you. I turned thirty last month, on February 2nd."

Adesua raised her eyebrows slightly. "Really? Happy belated birthday, then!" She said with a grin.

"Thank you." He replied.

She asked how he celebrated, and he shared the details with her.

When the call eventually ended, she checked her phone and found that they had spent about an hour and a half. She smiled. Something was definitely developing between them, and she asked the Lord to take control. "Defend Your interest in my life, Lord, in Jesus' name."

After service in church on Sunday, Pastor Mosun called her. "Tade told me that the two of you have been talking." Her voice was calm but direct.

Adesua confirmed it.

"I will tell you the same thing I told him." The pastor continued. "Both of you should take time to pray to be sure of what God is saying."

Adesua wanted to know her opinion.

"I have reasons to believe that God is involved, but it's important that both of you pray. I will also pray along with you."

Then she began to tell Adesua some of the things to consider, and questions she should find answers to. Adesua quickly brought out her iPad to take note of Pastor Mosun's advice. She didn't want to miss any detail.

When the pastor said she'd like to pray for her, Adesua knelt down and lifted her hands to receive the blessing.

****

As Tade kept in touch with Adesua, he found something interesting about her. Most ladies he knew liked to talk about hair and clothes, but Adesua discussed about the state of the nation, economic development, and helping people. He could also see that she was very passionate about children.

And as Adesua got to know more about him, she discovered that his vocabulary was better than hers, in conversation and writing, which she found interesting. Some of the men who were interested in her, she had to correct their spellings and grammars, which was a big turn off for her. Although, she guessed if she loved one of them, it wouldn't matter to her; she would correct with love.

About three months after, he said he would be coming to Nigeria, and she was excited about seeing him again. He arrived on Saturday, sixth of July, and went to his church on Sunday morning.

When he arrived at her house in the afternoon, she welcomed him warmly, ushering him into the living room. Her parents were there, and he greeted them respectfully.

Tade and Adesua sat down and began to exchange easy conversation.

As Adesua's parents looked at them and listened to them, they could see that they were in love. Adesua was happy, glowing. They also noticed that Tade was attentive and seemed protective of Adesua, and that made them very happy. *Thank You, Lord.* After some minutes, they got up and went to sit at the balcony.

Adesua had cooked, and after a few minutes, she brought out the food and set it on the lunch table, with necessary things. She invited him to the table, served him first, and then took a plate and served her own food. When they finished eating, they sat in the living room and watched a Christian movie together on the TV. Every now and then, they exchanged comments about the movie and laughed.

When he was leaving, he greeted her parents, and she saw him off. Outside, he made her know they'd need to talk. She didn't know what was on his mind, but somehow, she wasn't afraid.

She said she was free on Tuesday afternoon. "Does that work for you?"

"Sounds perfect."

She said she would return home around 1pm, and he said he'd pick her up at 2pm to go to a restaurant for lunch.

That day, she dressed carefully, and when he arrived and looked at her, his eyes told her that he thought she was beautiful.

When they finished eating, he began to talk. He said he had fallen in love with her and had been praying about her. "I want to build my life with you."

She admitted that she had fallen in love with him too and had been praying, but there were some things they would need to consider.

With a thoughtful expression on her face, she went on. "Let me just be straight up with you."

He leaned forward and listened carefully.

"I met a man at a time, whom I thought might be the right one for me, but shortly after we met, he began to complain that I worked with men and was too busy for his liking. He said he wasn't sure I wouldn't cheat on him, which I found very ridiculous. Some women may cheat on their spouses, but that's one thing I'll never do."

Tade smiled, his eyes never leaving hers. "Why have you brought this up?"

"I've brought it up so you can carefully consider everything and … well, to be sure." Her tone was steady but serious as she continued. "You know the kind of work I do. I have deadlines. There are times I work till late night. I work with men; I talk to men. Trust is important in every relationship, and especially in this. There are times I may not be able to attend some events with you, not because I don't want to, but because I am working. I wouldn't want my man to start comparing me with some other women or wives who show up at every event. I think you need to really think about that."

He smiled and asked gently, "You don't think I would have already thought about the kind of work you do?"

When she didn't respond, he spoke again, his voice reassuring. "As I said, I've prayed, and I know what I'm signing up for. And here's the thing, the kind of job you do or that I do is not the issue. If we both fear God and allow the Holy Spirit to lead us, we'd make the right decisions and would be fine."

As he looked at her, something occurred to him. Even though she was very capable, intelligent, and bold, he could see that she was also very tender; almost fragile, and he told himself that he'd protect and support her.

Taking a deep breath, she said, "Another issue to be considered is where we would live. You live in Ghana while I live here in Nigeria, and both of us have our careers. If we get married, one of us will have to relocate. How will we handle that?"

He took a deep breath. "Honestly, I've been thinking about it."

"I don't mind sacrificing for my husband, but in this case, I'm not sure that giving up what I'm doing is what God will want me to do. If God asks me to, I will, of course, but I don't think so."

He nodded to show understanding. After about a minute's silence, he said, "God will lead us, I'm sure. When we get to that river, we'll cross it."

"When would you like to get married?"

"I'm ready for marriage, maybe by the end of the year if it's okay by you." He answered.

"In that case, we have gotten to the river, and we need to decide what to do."

"Hmm. I'm settled in Ghana, and you're doing well here in Nigeria." He stopped and took a deep breath.

They talked back and forth, and at the end, he prayed that God would give them His solution.

"It's now in God's hand." Tade said confidently.

They sat in comfortable silence for a moment, and then he said, "Let's get to know more about each other. You mentioned that cheating is one thing you'd never do. What are the other things you wouldn't do?"

"Er -" Adesua considered the question but before she could respond, he spoke.

"Maybe I should go first. I don't cheat, and if we're meant to be together, I won't cheat on you, by God's grace. I'm a Christian, and my relationship with God is everything to me. I don't deceive or tell lies. If I do lie, I repent and make it right. And I won't take advantage of you."

When he stopped, Adesua nodded before she began to speak. "Well, I know I won't disrespect the man God leads me to marry. If, for any reason, I do, I'll apologize. I've learned a lot about respect from my parents and my pastors."

Tade smiled, appreciating her response. "That's awesome. Some wives don't realize how important respect is to their husbands."

He paused, then asked with genuine interest, "So, what are the things you will do?"

Adesua took a breath, then said, "I'll care for my family. I'll be busy sometimes with work or life, but I'll always love my family. Even when I'm unable to spend time with them, they'll always be in my thoughts. I'll make sure they never doubt how much they mean to me."

Tade listened carefully, nodding. "That's beautiful," he said. "Family is important. What about your likes and dislikes?"

Adesua smiled a little, appreciating the depth of their conversation. "Well, I keep my promises, so I like people who keep theirs. If someone can't keep a promise, I'd rather they tell me upfront than make me believe there's an agreement. I like punctuality, and I appreciate people who value time as well. I understand things happen sometimes, but it shouldn't be a habit."

Tade chuckled softly. "Punctuality is a good one. It says a lot about someone's respect for others."

As he began to mention his likes and dislikes, she listened, knowing they were laying the foundation for a lasting marriage. She prayed they would be able to overcome challenges and have a good marriage like her parents'.

While discussing how to have a strong and lasting marriage, they agreed that it would be important to stay away from behaviors that would undermine trust and respect, such as keeping secrets, abuse, and dishonesty. They also discussed the importance of clear communication, commitment to God, as well as supporting each other's spiritual growth always.

He also told her, "I know you're used to taking control because of the nature of your job. It's a trait I appreciate. But in our relationship, I want you to tone it down and trust me to handle things. If I'm not there, feel free to do whatever you need to do, but with me, I'd want you to enjoy being my wife."

She smiled, happy. "Okay, thank you."

He spoke again, "I can't help wondering sometimes how you didn't know that the Tony guy was deceiving you."

"I knew it, but I wanted to believe otherwise; I must admit that I was desperate to get married." She confessed.

When he said he'd want her to meet his father and brother, she hesitated.

"Shouldn't we resolve the issue about relocation first?" She pointed out.

"Don't worry about that, the Lord is in control and He will guide us." He said. "We can create time to discuss it with my aunt and her husband."

She agreed to meet his family the next day. "Do they know about me?"

"Yes."

She smiled, happy.

At home, she told her family that she had agreed to marry Tade, and they congratulated her.

The next day, she drove to Tade's house, and he opened the door for her. She stepped inside and saw his father and brother in the living room. They were standing, ready to greet her warmly, and she went to them.

Afterward, they sat down. She had told Tade she wasn't going to eat, and that juice or ice cream would be fine. He gave everyone a cup of ice cream, and then sat beside her.

Tade's father was looking at both of them, and he could see that his son was in love with Adesua.

He wanted to know when they intended to marry, and they said, "December, all things being equal." He nodded in approval, happy that one of his sons would be getting married soon.

On her way home, Adesua decided to talk to her father about their concern.

Her father was at home alone, in the living room. She greeted him and sat down. He wanted to know how the meeting went, and she told him that everything went well.

"I'd like to discuss something with you, Dad."

When he heard that, he put the newspaper in his hand down and looked at her with concern. "Is everything okay?"

"Yes, Dad." She assured him. "I just need your opinion on an issue we are trying to figure out."

"Okay. What's that?" He was focused on her, listening closely.

"You know, Tade lives in Ghana and works as a lawyer. He's doing really well there. Meanwhile, I have my TV show here, and I can't just pack everything up and relocate to Ghana when we get married. It's complicated."

Her father nodded, considering her words. "I see. And what does Tade think about all this?"

She sighed. "He's not sure, and we're praying about it. His main concern is that if he moves back to Nigeria, where would he even begin? He's already established in Ghana."

Her father leaned back in his chair, a thoughtful expression on his face. After a moment, he spoke calmly. "If that's his only concern, it shouldn't be a problem. I can help him. Tell him to see me."

Adesua's eyes lit up with hope. "Really?"

"Yes," her father said confidently. "Actually, your mother and I have been praying about who would take over the law firm when the time comes, as none of our children is a lawyer. Perhaps Tade is the answer to that prayer."

The following day, Adesua brought Tade to her father's office.

After some pleasantries, Adesua's father got straight to the point. "Tade, I've heard about your concerns regarding moving back to Nigeria, and I want to offer a solution. You can join my law firm. I'll start you off with a good salary, and I'll support you in any way I can to help you transition here. Of course, you will want to pray about it, but I think this might be an answer to you and Adesua's prayer."

Tade was taken aback by the generosity of the offer. He hadn't known how the conversation would go, but this was more than he expected. "Sir, I don't know what to say. Thank you, sir." He said, his voice filled with gratitude.

Adesua's father smiled. "You don't need to say anything right now. Just think and pray about it. But know that you're welcome here, and I'll help you establish yourself if this is the path you and Adesua choose."

Afterward, he began to ask Tade some questions so he would know how experienced he was, and how he could help him. As he listened to Tade, he could see that he was very intelligent, determined, hardworking, and focused. Above all, he was a Christian and he loved Adesua.

By the time Tade and Adesua were leaving the office, they felt like a burden had been lifted off their shoulders.

On Saturday, they attended a gospel concert, and the next day, he traveled back to Ghana.

Three weeks after, on Monday, the fifth of August, she traveled to Ghana to see him, and stayed in a guest house. He took her to his office, house, and then church on Wednesday. After the church service, he took her to his pastor and introduced her to him. The pastor asked them some questions and prayed for them.

On Friday, she was ready to return to Nigeria, and he came to the guest house, to drive her to the airport.

As she followed him to his car, she smiled. He was the right one for her. In her relationship with Jimi, she held back a lot. But not now. It was very clear to her now that she didn't love Jimi and that was why she struggled in the relationship, going back and forth.

Tade moved to Nigeria in October, and began working at Adesua's father's law firm. He rented a two-bedroom apartment in a nice neighborhood and furnished it modestly.

Their wedding day arrived on the third Saturday of December, and Adesua woke up feeling excited. She began to pray, giving glory to God for showing her mercy and granting her heart's desires. Her parents had money, and she had her own money. The only thing that had weighed on her mind was marriage, and now, God had answered her prayers.

In just a few hours, she would be joined in holy matrimony with the man she loved. Her parents had offered to cover all the wedding expenses, including her elegant wedding gown and Tade's black tuxedo, as a gift to both of them.

The church service began promptly at 11am, starting with the opening prayer, followed by the processional hymn, *Praise to the Lord, the Almighty, the King of creation.* On the arm of her father, Adesua began to walk down the aisle slowly, with grace and joy.

Before long, Tade and Adesua stood before Pastor Mosun's husband, the senior pastor of Solid Rock Bible Church, and began to exchange their vows.

"I, John Omotade Emmanuel, take you, Adesua Elizabeth Okalo, to be my wife, to have and to hold, from this day forward …

ALSO BY TAIWO IREDELE ODUBIYI

Fiction

In Love for Us
Love Fever
Love on the Pulpit
Shadows from the Past
This Time Around
Tears on My Pillow
Oh Baby!
To Love Again
You Found Me
My First Love
With This Ring
The Forever Kind of Love
What Changed You?
Too Much of a Good Thing
Is it Me You're Looking for?
Marriage on Fire
Then Came You
The One for Me
Sea of Regrets
Shipwrecked With You
Life Goes On
I'll Take You There
My Desire
If You Could See Me Now

When A Man Loves a Woman
Never Say Never!
Christmas to Remember
Accidentally Yours
She Who Has a Man
Comfort and Joy
Broken Together
Friends to Forever
One Day in December
Made a Way

For Children

Rescued by Victor
No One is a Nobody
Greater Tomorrow
The Boy Who Stole
Joe and His Stepmother, Bibi
Nike & the Stranger
Billy the Bully
Jonah's First Day of School
Bimbo Learns a Lesson

Nonfiction

30 Things Husbands Do That Hurt Their Wives
30 Things Wives Do That Hurt Their Husbands
Rape & How to Handle it
Devotionals for Singles

God's Words to Singles
God's Words to Couples
God's Words to Older Adults
Real Answers, Real Quick! (for singles)
Real Answers, Real Quick! (for couples)
Divine Instructions to live by – 1
Divine Instructions to live by – 2
God's Words to Women in Ministry
6 Hard Truths About Marriage & How to Handle Them

ABOUT THE AUTHOR

Taiwo Iredele Odubiyi is a pastor and the Executive President of TenderHearts Family Support Initiative, a Non-Governmental Organization, and Pastor Taiwo Odubiyi Ministries. She has a deep and strong passion for relationships and expresses this in ministries - nationally and internationally - to children, teenagers, singles, women and couples. She reaches out to these groups through counseling, seminars and programs such as Tenderheartslink, an online program for Christian singles and couples. Married and blessed with children, she is the host of the YouTube program – Tenderheartslink!

This is the thirty fifth of her soul-lifting and life-changing novels.

I love hearing from the readers of my books. If this book has blessed you, please send your comments to:
WhatsApp:+1(410)220-5676
Facebook: Pastor Mrs. Taiwo Odubiyi
        Pastor Taiwo Iredele Odubiyi's novels & books
Twitter: @pastortaiwoodub
Instagram: @pastortaiwoiredeleodubiyi

If you have friends and loved ones, then you do have people you should bless with copies of these very interesting and life-changing novels and books!